THE DOUBLE CHEESE BURGER MURDER

A Burger Bar Mystery Book 2

ROSIE A. POINT

Join my no-spam newsletter and receive an exclusive offer. Details can be found at the back of this book.

Cover by DLR Cover Designs
www.dlrcoverdesigns.com

 Created with Vellum

❧ 1 ❧

Bang, bang, bang!

A hammer clacked against the walls downstairs, knocking in nails and destroying my sleep in three fell blows.

I sat bolt upright in bed

"Hammer," I yelled. No, that wasn't right. I rubbed my eyes and blinked the sleep away. "Hammer? What's going on? Griz! Griselda!"

The shout woke Curly Fries, who leaped from my side with a hiss and a flick of her tail.

Footsteps stomped down the hall in my

best friend's house—dark at this hour of the night, and I kept on rubbing my eyes.

"Griz?" Gosh, my mouth was dry. "Griz, is that you making that noise? Girl, you'd better have a good explanation for this."

A shadowy figure appeared in my doorway. "How could that possibly be me?"

The blinking red numbers on my alarm clock caught my eye. "It's 4am. Why are you banging?"

"I'm not banging," she replied, as the hammering started up again.

It came in a pattern of threes from below.

"I'm not thinking right now." I got out of bed and stepped on Curly Fries' tail. She hissed and scratched my ankle. "Sorry!" But Curly had already streaked off into the darkness.

The hammer sounded again and realization struck me like, well, like a hammer between the eyes. This wasn't a case of impromptu home improvement on the part of

Griselda's annoying neighbor, Ray. This was someone at the front door.

"Who—who in their right mind?" I couldn't get the words out past the sleep. "Are you expecting guests?"

"Oh yes," Griz, my best friend, replied. "I always invite people over at the crack of dawn."

"No need to be sarcastic."

Grizzy headed off down the hall, and I followed her. Another bout of knocks started up.

"We're coming," I called, then lowered my voice to a grumble. "The nerve of people in this town. I swear, it's like they don't have any boundaries. If that's Mississippi I'm going to flip out."

"Even she's not this crazy," Griselda said.

Missi and Virginia were Sleepy Creek's most eccentric duo—old ladies who'd adopted gossip as their credo. They had a heart of gold a piece, but I'd rip it right outta Missi's chest if she'd disturbed my sleep for the scoop on old Mirabelle's top secret cobbler recipe.

I stepped on the back of Grizzy's sock, and she stumbled across the living room. She slammed into the front door. "Ouch."

"I want to be sorry," I said. "I just can't—"

"Shush, you." Griselda squared her shoulders and flicked on the porch and living room lights. "Who's out there?"

"Griselda?" A man's voice—throaty and a little feminine. "It's Jerry Lee Lewis."

My mind reeled. "Great Balls of Fire, Jerry Lee Lewis?"

"Don't be ridiculous," Griselda said. "He lives in Mississippi."

"Yes, because that's the ridiculous part. Wait, how do you know where Jerry Lee Lewis lives?"

Griselda shrugged. "I'm a fan."

"A fan. Of Great Balls of Fire? I mean, it's an OK song but I wouldn't go as far as to—"

"Uh, I can hear everything you're saying. I'm not *that* Jerry Lee Lewis. I'm your cousin. Jerry. Remember? We used to play pebble skips when we were kids?" the not-so-famous Lewis said, on the other side of the door.

"What's pebble skips?"

Grizzy rolled her eyes. "It's where you throw a pebble, skip to it, and the opposing player tries to hit you with pebbles while you skip."

"Your family is weird."

Jerry Lee coughed. "It's freezing out here."

"Shoot. Just a sec!" Griselda unlocked the front door and opened it for her cousin.

He wore an ascot. He was neat, with an unstained button-down shirt—white cotton but creased a little. Sitting down for a long period of time? And he carried a suitcase in one hand and a decorative wooden box tucked under his left arm.

If I'd been any form of awake, the details probably would have made sense.

"May I come in?" he asked.

"Of course," Grizzy said. "Of course." She stepped back and Jerry Lee tramped into the living room.

He placed his suitcase behind the sofa, then ever so carefully lifted that decorative cube and set it on the entrance hall table.

"Jerry Lee, I haven't seen you in years." Griz broke the quiet.

"Yes," he replied, and ruffled his blonde curls. "I've been on the road, as I'm sure you've heard, and that road has brought me right through Sleepy Creek." He pushed out a breath. "Kinda nostalgic being in this house again. It still smells like your mom's cooking."

"That's all on Griselda," I said. "She's a fantastic cook." I extended my hand. "Sorry, I don't think we've met. I'm Christie. I'm visiting from Boston."

"A pleasure." He had a soft palms and a gentle shake.

"Let's go through to the kitchen." Griselda straightened her robe. "I could use a cup of Joe. How about you?"

"Yes, please."

A cup of Joe, eh? So much for the last vestiges of sleep. The day had officially started with the less interesting version of Jerry Lee Lewis arriving on our doorstep. I couldn't help wondering how this day would end. Probably, with Curly Fries victimizing me for stepping on her tail.

In the week or so since I'd moved to Sleepy Creek, I'd learned that the wrath of Griselda's cat was swift and vicious. And that it ate more food than I could in a single sitting.

Curly Fries was the perfect ambassador for Sleepy Creek. Everyone in this town had a famous appetite.

We entered the kitchen and took positions at the centered table. I balanced my chin in my palm and studied Jerry through bleary eyes, as Griz flitted around, making coffee and being far too chipper for this hour of the night.

"What brings you to our neck of the Sleepy woods?" I asked.

"Oh, well, I'm an antique dealer, you see. I travel around to local stores and sell them

pieces they enquire about via my website."
Jerry twirled his wrists. Was it just me or did
he have a fake British accent? "I received a request from a store in Sleepy Creek. Terrible
Two's Antiques."

"No way," Griselda said. "That's Missi and
Virginia's store."

"You're kidding," I replied. "They own an
antique store?" How was that even possible?
Those two spent more time in Griselda's
Burger Bar than should've been legal.

"Yeah, they have an assistant working for
them, so they get to take time off. Missi has a
real passion for antiques," Griz said.

"Then I'm glad I came all the way out
here." Jerry smiled.

"Was that what the box was?" I asked.
"That cube thing?"

"That is a Civil War Era Writing box," he
said. "Officers used them for correspondence
during the war. Unfortunately, none of the ink
bottles or implements were intact, but it's still

a piece of history. I'm hoping it will take this Missi's fancy."

"Goodness," Griz said, and brought out three mugs. "That's fascinating."

"Where did you get it?" I couldn't imagine anything like that would come cheap or be readily available for purchase. My brain had finally revved its engines.

"Over in Cleveland at an auction. Gorgeous pieces on display, I'll tell you, but that one really caught my eye. Thanks." He accepted the cup from Griz and glugged down the coffee. "I'm excited to make the sale, but I'll be sad to see it go at the same time."

"How many offers did you get for it?" I asked.

"Quite a few. But the Sleepy Creek one was first and the highest. It seems this Missi person is really interested." Jerry Lee gave a happy sigh. "I love it when my pieces go to good homes."

Griz gave me my coffee then sat down

with hers at the table. "Here's an idea," she said. "Why don't we go to the store with you?"

"That would be great. I haven't been there before."

I downed my coffee and burned the back of my throat. My eyes watered. *Brilliant move, Christie.* "What time does it open?"

"Oh, at 8am, I think," Griz replied.

"In that case I'm going to—"

"Oh, no you don't." Griselda waggled her finger at me. "We're going to start the day with some chores, just like we planned yesterday."

"But—I—sleep?"

"Nope." Griselda grinned, and, for a moment, she looked a lot like Curly. "And I'll whip us up a BLT sandwich after we're done."

My stomach grumbled. "All right. You've got me there." I couldn't resist the offer of one of Grizzy's BLTs. "Where do we start?"

2

I yawned my way into Virginia and Missi's antique store—affectionately named Terrible Two's Antiques—and positioned myself to one side of the counter, so I could rest my tired head against the frilly wallpaper.

"Don't be such a drama queen," Griz whispered, as she swept by.

I responded with another yawn, covering it with my palm.

We'd managed to clean the house from top to bottom in the few hours since Jerry Lee

Lewis had turned up on our doorstep. I hoped to never see another batch of laundry again.

It wasn't that I didn't want to pull my weight around the house. It was that I didn't want to pull my weight at the crack of dawn. But Grizzy was the boss, both at work and in her own home, and I'd do what I could to help out.

Jerry Lee Lewis walked to the counter on Griselda's heels, carrying that fantastic specimen from the Civil War era. Between window cleaning duties, raking the yard and loading the dishwasher, I'd taken a peek at its polished outside. It was a thing of beauty.

He swaddled it in his arms and smiled at the elderly ladies, Missi and Vee, who gave him two very different onceovers. Virginia's brimmed with interest, and Missi looked as if Jerry Lee had brought in something nasty from outside and rolled it onto the front desk.

Or maybe Jerry Lee was the nasty thing *we'd* brought her.

"And who are you?" Missi asked.

"Don't be rude, sister. You must excuse her. She hasn't had her coffee yet."

"Maybe if somebody hadn't broken the coffee machine." Missi jerked her thumb in Vee's direction. "I wouldn't be in this predicament." She planted her butt on the stool beside the bronze cash register then cast an appraising look in my direction.

I was too tired to shrink back from her gaze. I'd witnessed drug deals gone bad and investigated homicides up in Boston. Last week I'd helped—partially hindered—the local police solve a murder that may have involved the Somerville mafia.

This woman scared me more than all of that.

Her sharp blue eyes bored into my soul. "Get that cat yet?"

I ignored her. The first thing Missi had ever said to me was that cats were great at clean up. They ate you if you died of natural, or not so natural, causes.

"Good morning, Miss Waters. And, eh, Miss Waters." Jerry Lee adjusted his ascot.

"Morning, dear," Virginia replied. "What can we help you with? That's a fine piece you're holding."

"Yes. My name is Jerry Lee Lewis. You contacted me about acquiring this antique and I've come to deliver it," he said, softly.

Missi perked up. "Great balls of fire," she said. "Now that's better than a cup of coffee. That's the writing desk, yes?"

"Yes, ma'am. The very same."

Missi slipped off her seat and practically teleported to Jerry Lee's side. She took the box from him and ran her hands over the top of it. "Magnificent," she said. "Just magnificent. Boy, you and I are going to have a long-standing relationship if you keep up deliveries of this quality."

Jerry Lee didn't look entirely sure how to take that. "I—all right."

Virginia removed the field writing desk from her sister's stroking fingers and carried it to one of the tables. "Missi dear, please take Mr. Lewis into the office and pay him for the antique. Make sure to create the invoice as I showed you."

"I'm not an idiot, Virginia," Missi sniffed —but her mood had definitely improved. She beckoned to Jerry Lee and stomped off down the aisle, past a worn but polished armchair and a display of Delft porcelain in a glass cabinet.

Jerry gave us a last glance then scurried after her, ascot flapping.

"This is wonderful," Virginia said, standing in front of the box. "Such a gorgeous piece."

"I'm glad you're happy with it," Griselda replied. "Jerry Lee turned up before the sun has risen this morning. He was super excited to deliver it to you two."

I tuned out the chatter and pushed off from the wall. Wandering feet brought me into the center of the store, and I lost myself between ancient books, their spines faded and coated in a thin layer of dust, and antique pans, vases, shelves and desks. The place smelled of teak and polish and the tang of wood straining against old age.

A crystal sculpture caught my eye—a translucent woman in a flowing dress that clung to her curves. A yellowing label had been attached to her base—Missi's illegible handwriting was scrawled across it.

This store hadn't been here when I'd first moved to town. But my mother, as practical as she had been, had loved places like this. Little shops with hidden treasures. There was a sense of adventure about this place, and I loved that.

"Christie?" Griselda called. "Have you fallen through the looking glass? We've got to get to the Burger Bar and open up."

Virginia made an appreciative noise. "What's the special this week, dear? More jalapenos?"

"No, we decided to go classic after all that spice and excitement." Grizzy's voice carried from the front, and I wound toward her. I popped out at the other side of the room, furthest from the entrance, just as another customer entered—one I recognized from my time in Sleepy Creek High School.

Blonde, short hair and expressive brown eyes. Beauty spot beside her nose. She had spilled a drop of toothpaste on her lapel. Toothpaste, huh? In a hurry? To get to an antique store? Why?

"Morning," she said.

"Haley." Griselda turned to the newcomer. "How are you? It's been over a week."

"Fine," Haley replied, and toyed with her fingers. I noted the behavior out of habit. She would press her thumb to her finger, encircle it then repeat the action. "I've been out of town but I'm back now."

Out of town. And the first place she visited was the antique store? Of course, I was reading too much into this. She was just another Sleepy Creek resident. My investigative habits kicking in. It didn't help that there had been a murder in town last week.

"It's wonderful to see you again, dear," Virginia said. "We've missed you. Have you come to buy or sell?"

"Sell," I said, then jammed my mouth shut.

All three women whipped their heads around, three sets of eyes and furrowed brows directed at me.

"Sorry. Didn't mean to interrupt."

"Is that—is that Christie Watson?" Haley lifted her hand to shield her eyes from the non-sun. A weird gesture. Overly dramatic. "I haven't seen you since high school."

"Yeah, time hasn't treated me well, has it?" I ran my hand through my hair. I'd left it loose today, and I still hadn't taken care of those split ends. A week on sabbatical and there'd been very little vacationing. "You look great, though."

"Thank you." Haley dusted off her shoulder.

The office door swung open, and Jerry Lee bustled out, grinning like Curly Fries after a hefty bowl of kibble. Missi followed with a spring to her step—it had been a successful transaction, then.

Missi caught sight of Haley. "Ah, there you are Haley. Our prodigal art dealer has returned. Where have you been, dear?"

"I had to—uh, family stuff."

"You had to family stuff? That's as clear as mud." Missi moved in behind the counter again. "We've had to find another antique expert to substitute for your deliveries. Meet Jerry Lee."

Haley gave Griz's cousin the stink-eye.

"Good morning," Jerry said, and smiled at her, hesitantly.

Haley didn't do him the courtesy of a reply. Apparently, the art and antique dealing biz was competitive. "What did you get from him?" Haley asked Virginia.

"That gorgeous field writing desk." Vee pointed to the item in question. "Feel free to take a look, dear, I know you're an enthusiast."

Haley bowled Griselda out of her path and

stomped over to the carved wooden box. What was this woman's problem? She'd gone from shy and sweet to shark infested waters in two seconds. Then again, money did strange things to people.

"This is it?" Haley skewered Jerry Lee with a look. "This is the best you can do?"

"I'm sorry," Jerry said. "Do I know you? You seem..."

"Angry," I put in. "Livid, actually."

"Butt out." Haley pressed her fingers to the clasp on the writing desk, and a clack echoed through the store.

I blinked. "Butt out of what?"

Haley opened the top of the writing desk and a strange noise hissed from the box.

Whisk-thunk!

"Ow!" She snatched her hand back. "What the—?"

"What happened?" I asked.

Haley held out her thumb and showed off a single bead of blood against the whorls of her skin. "There's a—There's a—" she said, and swallowed reflexively. "A needle in the box. There's a needle."

"Dear?" Virginia squeaked.

Griselda had gone pale.

"Call an ambulance." I moved to Haley's side just as the woman collapsed. I caught her and stumbled away from the antique. "Griz, call an ambulance."

"He's killed me." Haley's face drained of color. "I always knew he would find a way in the end."

"Stay with me, Haley."

Grizzy had her phone to her ear and yammered into it. Missi shook her head. Virginia was wide-eyed and gripping handfuls of plum fluffy hair. And Jerry? He turned on his heel and sprinted from the store.

"Hang in there, Haley," I said.

But it was too late. She was already gone.

𝕵 3 𝕽

D etectives Cotton and Balle arrived on the scene after the ambulance. They guided all four of us out of the antique store and into the harsh morning light. Virginia clung to Missi, who had never been this quiet in the time I had known her. Granted, that wasn't long, but still.

"Are you all right?" Arthur Cotton, Griselda's greatest admirer, stood next to her. "I'm sorry you had to witness that."

"I'm—I don't know," she said.

I ran my finger along my bottom lip and

held back the slew of questions that had already cropped up. I worked them over in my mind, searching for an answer. Another murder in Sleepy Creek, and so soon after the last one.

Something was up.

"Miss Watson." Detective Balle blocked my view of the street and the wrought iron lamps that lined it. "Why is it you're at the scene of every crime I investigate?"

"Bit of an overstatement," I said. "I wasn't there when you responded to the disturbance at Maura Joseph's house the other night."

"How did you know about that?"

"News travels fast." Maura's cat had gotten into an argument with her neighbor's dog, and that had led to a full-scale code red. People calling into the police station, convinced another murderer was on the loose.

Everyone was paranoid after last week.

But they had a good reason for it.

Poor Haley.

She hadn't stood a chance. The antique

box had contained a syringe filled with poison. It had to be poison. Something strong that acted quickly. Cyanide? Arsenic?

"All right, Miss Watson. It's best if you and I have a talk. Right this way," Balle said, and led me away from Grizzy who nodded and listened to what Arthur had to say, and Vee and Missi, who were pale but recovering from the shock.

He gestured to a bench on the sidewalk beneath a lamppost. All across the street, folks appeared in the doorways of their quaint brick-faced stores, peering out at the commotion. I took a seat, and Liam joined me, notepad and pen out.

"Do you want to walk me through what happened?"

"The victim entered the antique store at a quarter past nine in the morning. That's an approximation. She spent five minutes speaking to people in the store, then walked to the antique writing box and opened it. A syringe deployed. She died minutes later."

Balle scanned my face. An emotion I couldn't quite place flickered in his eyes. "Christie," he said. "Talk to me like you're a witness, not my partner. Cold facts are good but I'm much more interested in your take on what happened."

"Why?"

"Because you might've seen something the others didn't," he replied. "That's your job. And if you're anything like me you don't switch off when you're out of uniform."

He was right. I hadn't switched off in years. Whether it was a case I had a hand in, or my mother's cold case, I was always thinking about finding the truth.

It was a pity I didn't have any answers about my mom, and I hadn't gotten the chance to ask Balle for access to the cold case file either. Now wasn't the time.

"Christie?"

"Yes," I said, at last. "All right. OK. Haley came into the store, and she seemed angry. At first she was fine, right? She acted shocked to see me, but I wouldn't have called her behavior out of the ordinary."

"Did that change?" Balle clicked his ballpoint. He scraped the end along the stubble on his square jaw.

"Yes. The minute she spotted Jerry Lee. Or maybe it was the minute Virginia told her that they'd purchased something from him."

"Jerry Lee?"

"Yeah, that's Griselda's cousin. He ran out of the store right after Haley collapsed."

"What's his full name?"

"Jerry Lee Lewis," I said.

Balle's bottom lip twitched. He wrote the name down but didn't comment. "And he sold the box to Virginia and Mississippi?"

"Yes. It's a Civil War era writing desk. They contacted him via his website and he brought it down from Cleveland to deliver it to them."

"Right." Balle wrote that down too. His handwriting was a series of neat, square strokes. Every movement was precise.

I told him what had happened next, the minor disagreement, and Haley's insistence on examining the box. "I think it was spring-loaded or something. The syringe, you know? The minute she opened the box it struck her." It had reminded me of a coiled viper, waiting to lash out.

"I'll need to speak to this Jerry Lee guy," Balle said, and unclicked his ballpoint. "Do you know where he's staying?"

"No," I said. "He's just come to town, I think. That's what he told us this morning when he turned up at Griselda's place."

"I'll get more information from Miss Lewis."

"Yeah, she probably has his phone number." I touched Liam's arm, and a rush of sparks traveled over my skin. I drew my hand back again and placed it in my lap. "Whoever loaded that box had to either know Haley was going to open it or expected Jerry Lee to."

Balle nodded. "Don't worry, Miss Watson. The Sleepy Creek Police Department has this under control." He rose and effectively dismissed any further discussion. Clearly, the good detective didn't want me involved in this case either.

Just because I'd helped with the last one, didn't mean I could do the same this time around.

Balle walked toward Griselda and Arthur, but spared me a single glance. Was it a warning? He was somber at the best of times, so I couldn't tell the difference between serious investigative mode and a non-verbal threat for me to butt out of his investigation.

"Butt out," I muttered. Exactly the words Haley had used shortly before someone had injected her with poison. "Got to be cyanide. Instant. Got to be—"

"Are you OK?" Griselda plopped down beside me on the bench. "That was ... I don't even know how to put it."

"Me neither" I said. "But, you know what this means, right?"

"I get the feeling you're about to tell me."

She sighed and pinched the bridge of her nose. She had to be tired too, and we still had to get to the Burger Bar and open up.

"Either Jerry Lee did this or someone who wanted to murder Jerry Lee," I said.

"How do you figure that?"

"Well, Jerry Lee had to know that someone would open that box. Perhaps, he knew that Haley would be there. He spring-loaded it and when it happened, he freaked and ran out."

"We're not super close, but that is my cousin you're talking about, Chris. I'd like to give him the benefit of the doubt." Grizzy's voice shook. Now probably wasn't the best time to discuss this.

My cop brain had already started working overtime, and I couldn't shut it off. "Sorry," I said. "Sorry, Griz. I'll shut up, now."

"It's OK. I understand. I just—why do *you* think he ran out?"

Apart from the obvious? "I can't say. Maybe he got spooked." I stood up. "Griz, I need to go home and take a shower before we open up. Is that OK?"

"Of course," she said. "I'm going to head over to the Burger Bar."

"You don't want to take the day off?"

"No. No, definitely not. If I take the day off I know I'll sit at home and think about the murder. I need to work. And I need to be there in case Jerry Lee comes in to talk. He hasn't answered his phone since he left, and I've tried calling like twenty times."

"If you're sure." I shared her feeling about the work taking our minds off this particular event. I could only hope that the awesome atmosphere in Griselda's Burger Bar would override the questions.

I couldn't afford to get in trouble. I'd lucked out the last time, but if I stepped too far over the line again, I could bet my bottom dollar that Balle would call Chief Wilkes and get me fired for good.

"Besides, I get the feeling Virginia and Missi are going to need two servings of the double thick choc malts today." Griz pointed at the terrible twins beneath their Terrible Two's Antiques sign.

Detective Balle spoke with them while Detective Cotton pulled a police line across the front of their beloved store.

4

I sat on the stool at the counter in Grizzy's Burger Bar and avoided my reflection in the mirror behind it. I had run a brush through my hair after my shower, but I had foregone mascara—my mother's infamous secret weapon.

The circumstance warranted it, though. The brunch rush hadn't started yet, so I didn't have much to take my mind off things, and the presence of the terrible twins in their corner booth didn't help much either.

They cast glances around the inside of the

restaurant, whispered to each other, and acted as if the shadows held secrets. I didn't blame them. Sleepy Creek wasn't exactly 'murder central,' and we'd had two of the things in the span of a month.

"Hear anything yet?" I asked Grizzy, who fiddled with the mixer above the bar fridge.

She'd already whipped up two choc malt shakes for the ladies, but she hadn't quit cleaning or moving since she'd gotten in. She had even tried to impose her presence in the kitchen, only to be kicked out by Jarvis.

"Nothing. Not even a text message." Grizzy polished the coffee machine next, her rag *thwapping* against the plastic and metal. "It's ridiculous. He turns up at my house in the dead of the night with that murder box and then—"

"Murder box?" A dumpy woman with hair as yellow as the early morning sun strode up to the counter. Short, messy. She had a red stain in the corner of her mouth, possibly ketchup, or a cheap shade of red lipstick she'd removed for the safety of the eyesight of Sleepy Creek's residents.

Griz and I had been so involved in our conversation we hadn't noticed the front door's clatter.

"So, it's true then." The newcomer whipped off a silken scarf and used it to dust off one of the bar stools. She took a seat after she was done and dumped the accessory in her lap. "Haley Combes is dead."

"And a pleasant morning to you too, Mona."

Mona. The name was meant to be said in a throaty growl, teeth clenched and palms a-sweatin'. Mona Jonah had a reputation in Sleepy Creek as the worst, the foulest gossip to walk down Main Street.

Her quaint name did nothing to soften her nasty attitude.

I hadn't spoken to her before, but, boy, the rumors about the Gossip-in-Chief circulated through the store with centrifugal force.

"Yes, darling, lovely to see you out and

about. Is it true you're dating Arthur Cotton, now? He's investigating Haley's death, yes?"

Wow. Mona's reputation didn't do her justice. "I'm Christie," I said, and extended my hand.

She took it with fingers tipped in nails that put mountain lions to shame. "Oh, I know who you are. Everyone knows who you are. You're the Bostonian."

"I'm—I guess you could say that, yeah."

The woman's grip tightened, a stranglehold, and I returned it with force. I'd never been one to back down from a challenge. She pulled free. "Back to Arthur Cotton," she said, and pursed her lips.

"Arthur's a friend." Griselda managed to keep a straight face, though I didn't know for how much longer Arthur would remain a friend. He'd asked to speak to Griz in private a few days ago, but life had been busy, as had the restaurant.

He wanted to ask her out on a date.

"A friend." More lip pursing and appraisal ensued.

"Can I get you something to eat, Mona? We've got a special this week."

"What is it?" the woman asked, though she didn't appear interested in burgers.

"Jarvis has created the Double Cheese Burger."

"A cheeseburger."

"No, a Cheese Burger," Griz replied. "He was adamant about that. He layers the sesame bun with two thick, juicy patties, grilled to perfection, with a total of four slices of Monterey Jack between 'em."

My mouth watered. "Wow."

Even Mona swallowed. The gossip stalled on her tongue, and the scent of flame grilled meat drifted from the open kitchen window on cue. Jarvis whistled inside, no doubt whipping up his pre-brunch rush snack.

The man never tired of burgers, and, the way he made them, I couldn't blame him.

"And that's not all." Griselda licked her

lips. "It's layered with sauces of your choice, barbeque, ketchup, mustard, you name it, and topped with pickles and fried onions."

"I'll have one. Hold the onion and the embalmed cucumbers." Mona picked up her scarf, shook it off then fastened it around her throat again.

She had to be in her early forties, but the woman's attitude spoke of years beyond that. It was as if she'd seen everything there was to see.

"Coming right up." Griz walked to the kitchen window and dinged the bell. "One Double Cheese Burger and hold the good stuff, Jarvis."

"Comin' right up, mon," Jarvis called back.

I was tempted to ask Griselda to order one for me too, but I had a strict rule about eating during work hours. If I let myself, I'd eat one burger for every basket I served to the patrons, and that would end with me rolling out of the front doors at the end of every shift.

"Don't think you've distracted me with

food, Griselda Lewis. I want the details. And you know I'll get the details." Mona clicked her claws on the countertop. "Now, would you like to present the facts or would you prefer it if someone else gave me a garbled version of the truth to disperse?"

"Last I checked you weren't a police officer, Mona. Nor a member of the press. Why do you have the right to disperse anything?" Griz asked.

"This isn't about rights." Mona waved her hand as if the topic was an irritant. "It's about delivering the right message to the right people. Folks in Sleepy Creek will want to know what happened. It would be a shame if they got the wrong idea. You know, like the idea that maybe the terrible two were involved in the murder of a young woman."

"That's a load of hot trash, and you know it," I said.

Mona turned cool eyes on me. "I don't know anything yet. Other than the fact that it's a murder. Officially, it's being called a murder. Oh, and I know that you two were there. You witnessed her death."

"This is fantastic mealtime talk," I said.

But the woman wasn't deterred. "Another rumor has it that your cousin, Jerry Lee, that he's the one who killed her. Now, I always thought Jerry was kind of effeminate, you know? The kind who—"

"That's enough." I slipped off the bar stool. "A woman passed this morning and all you care about is a scoop for your gossip circle. Some of us have work to do in here. You clearly don't, unless you class being a Grade A nuisance as a job."

Mona stiffened. "Is this how you treat your customers Griselda? I heard this was what Loopy Paul went through before he died in your back yard."

She was unbelievable. A train that couldn't be stopped, and, if we let her, she'd smash right into the back wall and ruin brunch.

Jarvis 'tinged' the order in the window, and Grizzy hurried to fetch it. She slid it into place in front of Mona. "Order up," she said.

"It looks delectable." Mona studied the burger. "Pity the atmosphere in here is so cold." She got up and left her basket behind, the burger steaming delightful vapors. She paused halfway across the restaurant and looked back at us. "I don't have to tell you you'll regret this, Griselda." And then she clanged out of the restaurant and into the spring air.

"I've never been able to figure her out," Griselda said. "She wants to gossip, but I've never understood why. Maybe it makes her feel powerful."

"Or maybe she's pulling strings we can't see."

"You're just paranoid." Griz gestured to the burger. "Why don't you take that out back and finish it off? It's not technically work hours if there's no one to serve, right?"

"You're incorrigible." But I didn't argue. I took the burger and my thoughts outside.

Possibilities swirled through my head, matched by an equal number of questions about my mother, about Haley's death.

I'd come to Sleepy Creek seeking peace and a bit of quiet. Sure, I might've had an ulterior motive regarding my mother's case, but, at this rate, I would never get a moment of relaxation.

I took a huge bite of the burger and consoled myself with the rich, wholesome flavors and the softness of that bun.

I'll get to the bottom of this one too. Just you wait.

5

Griz squealed into my bedroom—the ever pink and floofy guestroom in her home—at half past seven that evening and hopped from one bare foot to the other. "He's coming!" she yelled. "He's coming."

Curly Fries leaped from my pillow onto my head. She gave a yowl and scrape-jumped onto the top of the dresser. "What the—? Ow!"

"He's coming, Christie. I'm going to have a heart attack. Or an embolism. Or one of those cathartic respiration thingies."

THE DOUBLE CHEESE BURGER MURDER

"Cardiac respiratory arrest?" I asked. "That's a horrible thing to say." Was Jerry Lee on his way?

"I know, and I don't care." Grizzy massaged her chest and marched back and forth in front of my bed. "Arthur just called me. He said he was sorry he didn't get to speak to me in person but things have been crazy lately and that he needs to blow off steam and that he wants to go out and grab a bite to eat."

"Whoa, that's a lot of conjunctions."

"He's coming. In like, a half an hour. I'm going to lose it, I swear."

"Why didn't you postpone the date until tomorrow?" I massaged the scratches on my scalp. Curly Fries peered over the lip of the dresser door, her yellow eyes shameless.

"Are you kidding? I've been waiting forever for Arthur to ask me out and I know if I postpone it he's going to go all shy on me again, and we'll never get the chance. What do I wear? Chris, what do I wear?"

"Relax, woman. Don't make me shake

you." I closed the book I'd been reading—an Agatha Christie mystery because they reminded me of mom. "Let's get organized. We have to approach this from a tactical perspective. Assess all our options and move forward in an educated—"

"It makes me crazy when you talk like that. Come on, Chris. He's coming!"

"Fine, fine. Where are you going to eat? Let's start there."

"He didn't say, but there are only really two choices in town. My burger bar, which is closed, and Sal's Pizzeria," she said. "There's the Never-Do-Well Bar too, but that's not any kind of food I'd like to eat, and I don't think he'd take me there."

"Right. And what's the dress code like at the pizzeria?"

"Casual. Family dining."

"So you won't be breaking out the ball gowns." I scratched the underside of my chin. "I'm thinking something understated. A spring dress or a pair of skinny jeans and a loose blouse."

"Got it!" Griselda streaked out of the guestroom before I could give my humble opinion on makeup—probably a good thing since I hadn't had too much experience in that department. She'd laugh at me if I brandished my mascara wand and nothing else.

I sat on the edge of the bed again and considered the paperback, picked it up, smoothed my fingers over the worn cover. Once, long ago, I'd thought about guys the way Griselda did now. I'd been excited at the prospect of meeting a man I could settle down with, but then I'd started focusing on my career.

I was married to mystery.

I wanted nothing more than to find the next clue, the next answer, and, every time I did, it was as if a tiny piece of a bigger puzzle clicked into place.

The puzzle was *supposed* to paint the picture of Christie Watson. It was supposed to show people the kind of woman I was, the kind of woman my mother would have been proud of.

But I wasn't sure about anything since I'd come back to Sleepy Creek.

"Here!" Griselda clamored across the boards again.

I tossed the paperback aside and looked up at my best friend then gasped. "Wow, Grizzy. That took you all of five minutes. You look amazing!"

"You're sure?" She swirled on the spot and her loose cotton dress flared around her knees —violet, a color that suited her complexion beautifully. "I didn't do much with my makeup. Shoot, I still have to do my hair and get a sweater."

"Take that cream cardigan of yours," I said.

"You're right. That's a brilliant idea." She rushed out again.

So much excitement and activity. It was good. It would take her mind off Jerry Lee and the investigation until she got home to tell me about her date with Cotton.

A knock rattled downstairs, followed by the sharp trill of the doorbell. "I'll get it," I called out.

"Yeah, you'll get it. I'm not ready yet. I can't believe he's this early. Gosh, I mean—" Grizzy's frantic diatribe dissolved into bangs and squeaks as she rifled through her things in the next room.

I chuckled under my breath and headed out of the guest room and down the stairs, through the kitchen and into the living room. A thought struck me. Why hadn't Jerry Lee hit the doorbell this morning? He'd sure banged loud enough to wake the neighborhood. I dismissed it as the desperate scratching of a tired mind. It couldn't mean anything.

I stopped at the front door and rested my fingertips on the latch. "Who's there?"

"This is Detective Balle."

"Ah." I drew back the latch and opened up

on the handsome detective. He had changed out of his uniform. Was this a personal visit? "Good evening, Detective Balle. How may I be of service?"

"I came to speak with Miss Lewis about her cousin," Balle replied.

"I'm sorry but Griz is kind of in the middle of something right now." I backed up a few steps, tilted my head and called out, "You can relax, girl. It's not him. It's the other one. Balle."

"Oh thank heavens," she yelled back.

"Am I missing something?" Balle asked.

"Come on in," I said. "I'll tell you about it over a cup of coffee and a cookie. Assuming you eat them."

"I'm a cop," he said. "Of course, I eat cookies."

I set out for the kitchen and the afore-mentioned sustenance. Balle sat down at the table in his plain clothes and jerked up the legs of his jeans. "What's going on? I assume Griselda isn't leaving town?"

"She's got a date with your partner in about oh, twenty or so minutes?" I busied myself with the coffee grounds. "You'll have to excuse her when she comes down. She'll be a nervous wreck."

"About time," Liam muttered.

"What was that?"

"I said it was about time. Those two have been dancing around the elephant in the room for months. I've tried speaking sense into Arthur, but he wouldn't hear it. I'm glad something finally gotten through to him."

"Not everyone's as good at seizing the day as you are, detective."

"That wasn't what I meant."

"Sure, it wasn't. Now, why don't you tell me the real reason you're here. You're wearing cologne and you ironed your shirt." I turned on him, still holding the spoon and the jar of grounds. "I'm pretty good at reading people and their motives, but I can't quite place you. I know you're a professional, and you wouldn't come here in plain clothes when you wanted to talk about something related to an ongoing investigation. That's not your style. So, what is it?"

Liam worked his jaw. "You got all that from my shirt and cologne?"

"And you shaved," I said. "You had stubble this morning."

He blushed bright red. "You seem to know an awful lot more than you should, Miss Watson."

"I observe. It's nothing weird." I spun to avoid his gaze and filled the machine with water to the mark, then clicked on the switch.

"I wanted to find out if Jerry Lee Lewis had come back to the house. We haven't been able to track him down."

"Maybe he skipped town," I mused, more to myself than to the detective. If he had, it would make Jerry look awful guilty.

"Not as far as we know. We traced his rental car to a lot on the other side of town, near Terrible Two's Antiques."

I mulled that one over. Liam still hadn't

told me why he'd really come, though. It couldn't be to talk about Jerry looking like that. So what was it? I opened my mouth to press the issue—

The doorbell rang again, and this time it had to be Arthur.

"Coming!" Griselda appeared in the doorway, glorious in that dress with her cardigan slung over her arm. "Coming. Oh, hello detective. I'm afraid I can't stay to talk. I've got a date."

"That's quite all right, Miss Lewis. We'll catch up tomorrow."

Tomorrow? Perhaps, Liam had come to ask Grizzy out too? But no, he surely wouldn't do that to his friend and partner? He wasn't that type of guy.

"Have fun." I waved at my best friend. "Don't get into too much trouble."

"Shush you." She swept past us into the living room then out of the front door with a *click, slam, bang.*

Liam cleared his throat. "I'd—uh. I'd better head out. Thanks for the hospitality."

"But ... the coffee?"

"Another time perhaps." He gave me the strangest look then, a half-frown-smile, before getting up. He spared me one last glance. "Take care, Christie." And then he was gone.

"What on earth was that about?" I whispered.

The coffee pot burbled an answer.

6

"Looks like it's just you and me tonight, Curly," I said.

The cat wasn't impressed—she flicked her tail twice and whapped it into her empty kibble bowl. She hadn't forgiven me for standing on her tail, even though I'd apologized profusely.

"Wow." I'd gone from hardened Boston detective to apologizing to cats. This was the legacy of Sleepy Creek.

Curly Fries gave a signature *prrt-meow* and whacked her tail against the bowl again.

"Kibble? Really? You ate like a half an hour ago. Sorry, cat, if I give you more food Griselda will kick my butt. She's already worried about your weight." Curly Fries wasn't the skinniest kitty on the block.

Griz and I held the firm belief that she'd found another food provider, possibly the old lady, Mrs. Immelmann, across the street.

Curly heaved herself off the tiles and waddled out into the hall, taking her sour attitude with her.

"We're going to have to put you on a diet, Curly."

The doorbell buzzed, and I pushed off from the counter, shuffled through to the hall. I'd ordered pizza fifteen minutes ago—no way had they arrived already, though I was looking forward to Sal's Fully Loaded Pizza for sure.

But if it wasn't the delivery guy, then who had come knocking? Had Detective Balle come back to question me again? The whole ironed shirt, cologne trick had set me on edge

—he was up to something, I just couldn't figure out what it was.

"Who's there?" The metal knob cooled my palm.

Scratching sounded against the wood, followed by a dull thump.

"Hello?" I longed for my weapon. "Announce yourself this instant."

"It's me," a man whispered.

"Who's me?"

"Me. Jerry Lee."

Well, I never. The missing man had turned up at Grizzy's house. She would be overjoyed.

"Just a second." I drew back the latch then let the murder suspect into the house.

Jerry Lee had gone from antique salesman to distraught homeless guy. He shuffled across the threshold, wringing his palms, his hair stringy and sticking up at odd angles. It kinda looked like he'd been electrocuted.

"Where have you been?" I measured my tone—I probably wouldn't get anything out of him if I was too rough. I locked up, twitched the curtain aside and checked that the coast was clear in the street. No handsome detectives in sight.

"I'm sorry." Jerry tugged on his dirt-streaked ascot. "I'm sorry. I panicked. I had to get out of there. I was afraid they'd think I'd done it, and I can't deal with that. I'm not a murderer, I swear. I would never hurt a soul, and I know that the cops won't take kindly to me because of—"

"Because of what?" I took his arm and guided him to the sofa. "Jerry Lee? Why don't you want to talk to the police? What happened?"

"I—look, Griselda doesn't know about this, and I didn't want her to ever find out. I thought if she knew what had happened she'd hate me for it or judge me."

"Slow down." I sat in the armchair opposite him. "Let's start from the top." Curly Fries wandered in and hovered nearby, studying the newcomer to her domain.

Jerry Lee shuddered a breath. "I left

Sleepy Creek years ago, and Griselda knows that. She doesn't know why I left, though."

"OK, so why *did* you leave?"

"I always had a passion for art, and when I was younger I was reckless. I broke—oh heavens, I broke into an art store in town and stole supplies. The police caught me and threatened me. They arrested me. I was a juvenile, and I got a slap on the wrist, but I'm sure they've never forgotten it."

Detective Balle was my age, though, and he wasn't originally from Sleepy Creek. He couldn't know about Jerry's history, or he hadn't until Jerry had run out, and he'd likely had to do a background check on him.

"Jerry, you need to speak to the police. The longer you stay away, the guiltier you look."

"They think it was me."

"I have no idea what they think, but this? This hiding? It doesn't look good." I didn't buy his explanation for why he'd run, though.

There had to be more to it than an embarrassing theft as a teen.

"All right," Jerry said. "Yes, I'll speak to them. Or—what if—?"

"Stop." I pushed my palm toward him. "I'll level with you here, Jerry. This doesn't look good for you. That was your antique, and there was tension between you and Haley in the store. You ran out after she was poisoned."

Jerry whimpered. "I would never—"

"The police will view you as a person of interest." He was the *only* person of interest at the moment. "I can help you, Jerry, you need to be honest with me. Tell me what happened."

"I don't know what happened. I didn't do anything wrong." A muscle twitched in his jaw.

I rolled the pads of my thumbs against each other. Jerry had to have information. Bottom line: a syringe full of poison had been attached to that box by someone.

Ye old civil war general hadn't put it in there.

"Do you want my help?" I asked.

"Your help? You'll hide me from them?"

"No, Jerry. I'm a cop."

"Wh-what?"

"I'm a detective. I'm from Boston, and I'm here on vacation. I can help find the person who did this."

Jerry gripped the arm of the sofa with both hands and dug his nails into the fabric.

"For heaven's sake, calm down," I said. "I don't care that you stole art supplies. I'm trying to get to the bottom of this case." Uh oh. This case. The bottom of it. The words had popped out before I could stop them.

Detective Balle would hang me out to dry if I interfered again, and this time I didn't have an excuse. My mother's murder wasn't involved. I should've focused on that case instead of Jerry's little problem. The tug of intrigue was too great.

I'd never handled a case of spring-loaded

poison injection via antique writing desk before.

Jerry hadn't stopped harassing the sofa.

"All I need is answers, Jerry. Listen, I'm Griselda's best friend, and I don't want to see her upset. I'll do what I can to help you, but you need to answer my questions. Understand?"

His chin shifted up and down.

"Good. Now, talk to me about that box. You said you got it in Cleveland?"

"Yes. At an antique auction."

"Did you open the box at any point?" I asked.

Jerry did another chin shift. "Just after I bought it. I hoped there'd be ink bottles or papers inside, that the auctioneer had missed them. No such luck."

"And there wasn't anything inside it then? No syringes?"

"No."

Curly Fries leaped onto the arm of my chair and planted herself on it. She gave Jerry the cat stare and ignored me completely. We were a united front—a show of cat-human strength in the face of Jerry Lee Lewis' strange behavior and stench. Where had he been, the sewers?

"Did you leave the writing box alone at any point?"

"Not since Cleveland."

"But you did leave it alone in Cleveland," I said.

"Yes. In the hotel room. I left it there that evening and ran down to check my mail at the front desk," Jerry said. "I was gone for five minutes at the most."

"Have you opened the box since then?"

"No."

Assuming Jerry hadn't just fed me—and Curly—a pack of lies, that was our window. The murderer had to have entered Jerry's hotel room and planted the syringe during that period. But it was touch and go. Too risky.

Why would the murderer have placed it in

the box at that point if the target was a Sleepy Creek resident? Unless Jerry Lee had been the target, and the murderer had seen it as a matter of time before Jerry opened the box again.

"Do you have enemies, Jerry?" I asked.

He resumed a white-knuckled grip on the sofa. "One accumulates certain adversaries in the antiques game. I suppose you could say that I had some enemies. Other salesmen or people who bid on the box, perhaps. You don't think that the murderer—that they were trying to kill me, do you?"

"I can't say for certain." It was a distinct possibility. "Did you know Haley well?"

"Not at all. I'd never met her before ... before today."

If someone had been after Jerry, I had to narrow down the suspect list from 'everyone in Cleveland.' But was that really the answer?

Haley's last words had been telling.

She'd mentioned that someone had wanted to kill her. A man.

THE DOUBLE CHEESE BURGER MURDER

I chewed on my bottom lip.

Why use Jerry to get to her? Why do it that way? Unless the murderer had wanted to use Jerry as a scapegoat? Surely, Haley would have called out Jerry's name if he had been the murderer, instead of just saying 'him?'

The next logical step would be to work out Jerry or Haley's list of natural enemies. Folks who bid on antiques at the auction, other antique salesmen or collectors. Now, who would know people like that? Who would connect with them on a daily or weekly basis?

"Vee and Missi," I whispered.

"What was that?"

If I spoke to the terrible two, I might be able to formulate a list of potential suspects and cross reference them with Jerry's natural antique enemies. And Jerry's enemies would be Haley's as well. They were in the same business.

This was the best lead I had, short of calling every auction house in Cleveland.

My gut told me that this *had* to do with

Sleepy Creek. Either the murderer had been sloppy and decided that whoever opened the box needed to die, or they'd been a genius and planned the death of Haley from afar.

Or it was Jerry who'd orchestrated the whole thing? Curly and I eyed him.

"What?"

"Why didn't you open the box again?" I asked. "After that first time."

Jerry blushed. "Because it was locked, and I couldn't find the key."

"But it was unlocked on the morning Haley opened it."

"Yes. I—I don't know how that happened. I never found the key. I negotiated the fact that it was locked with Missi and agreed to drop the price because of it," Jerry said.

I squeezed my eyes shut.

The box couldn't have miraculously unlocked itself. Someone had unlocked it. If Jerry hadn't left the box alone after leaving Cleveland—wait! The chores!

Griz, Jerry and I had gone outside to clean

the windows. We'd left the front and back doors unlocked. Was it possible that the murderer had snuck in and unlocked it while it was unattended?

That would've taken a great deal of stalking on his part—following Jerry's every move and plotting the murder all the while.

The front door's buzzer rang again, and Jerry let out a piggy squeal.

"Relax," I said. "It's the pizza. Why don't you go upstairs and take a shower, Jerry? We can talk about this over some grub." I lurched out of my seat, hungry for food and answers.

This was too messy.

Luckily, I loved a challenge.

❧ 7 ❧

I had a marshmallow on my face. A big, pillow-shaped marshmallow. I sneezed and white sugary dust puffed from my mouth. I inhaled and more of it clogged my throat. What on earth?

If this was a marshmallow, it sure didn't smell good. It smelled like—

My eyes snapped open, and I yelped.

It wasn't a marshmallow. It was Curly Fries!

The cat had taken up residence on my forehead, and her tail lay against my half-open lips.

"Geroff!" I spat out fluff.

She flicked her tail against my shut mouth, and settled herself on my forehead.

"Curly." I scooped her up and fed her onto the carpet in the living room. The old clock on the wall ticked, the mechanism clacking. It was past 11pm and Griselda wasn't home from her date.

Jerry had gone to bed ages ago, and the remains of our too cheesy pizza were locked up tight in a Tupperware in the kitchen. I didn't doubt Curly had sat on my head as an act of revenge.

I rubbed my eyes and forced myself upright on the sofa. "Do that again and you'll lose the tail."

She waved the offending appendage at me again—she knew it was an empty threat. I'd saved her once from the broom-smacking antics of Griselda's next door neighbor, Ray.

I shoved my hair out of my face then

got up and stretched, grabbed my phone off the coffee table. No messages from Griz.

If she didn't get home soon I'd have to give her a call to check in.

I'd seen too many happy nights go wrong in Boston. Too many pizza evenings or dates or family gatherings turned bad.

I shot a text to Griz's phone.

"Coming home before Christmas?"

I walked through to the kitchen—time to reheat some of that pizza—and my phone buzzed.

"Home in ten!" And she'd put a heart emoji on the end. Talk about enthusiastic. She'd obviously had a good night.

I dragged the pizza onto a paper plate and slammed it in the microwave then beep-booped the appropriate buttons.

Even the pizza hadn't calmed down Jerry. He'd been in semi-hysterics with his mouth full, an image I didn't wish upon my worst enemies. The guy was convinced the cops were after him for the crime he supposedly didn't commit.

"Don't be mean," I muttered.

I didn't have proof that Jerry had or hadn't done it, but my cop instincts dictated I had to follow every lead, not just the ones that would make Griselda comfortable.

The microwave pinged, and I brought out the pizza, then set it on the table—it would have to do for a late night snack and discussion. Coffee next.

A slam, and Griselda's happy humming drew me from the coffee pot.

"Hello, I'm home," she called out.

Curly Fries meowed at full volume.

"Shush, shush, baby, I know. Did you miss me?" Griselda tottered into the kitchen, the fat cat tucked into her arms. She smooched the kitty on the head, repeatedly. "I missed you, sweetie."

I rolled my eyes. "The only thing she misses is the opportunity to steal food."

"Such a meanie." Grizzy's hair was loose

around her shoulders and mussed by the breeze outside. "What?" she asked. "You're staring at me."

"Your button is loose. It wasn't before."

"Relax, mom, I hooked it on Arthur's car door," she said. "He was such a gentleman. He offered to sew it for me."

"Now I've heard everything. Cotton sews?" I snorted. "Cotton sews."

"Reel it in, Sleeping Beauty." Griz put down Curly Fries. The cat promptly stuck her nose in the air and began circling the table. She was the shark, the pizza was her prey, and heaven forbid whoever stood in her path.

I lifted the plate off the table, and she actually hissed at me.

"How did you know I was asleep?" I asked.

"Elementary my dear—"

"Don't you dare say Watson."

"Fine. Christie. You're not the only one who pays attention, you know. Also, you've got the sofa's pattern imprinted on your left cheek there." She pointed. "Why are you up so late?"

"Can't a friend worry about another friend without judgment?" I asked. "I reheated the pizza. And I'm about to make some coffee." I gave her the plate then sauntered to the pot.

"No, seriously. Why are you up this late? You've got the early shift at the Burger Bar tomorrow."

"Yes, boss." I clicked the switch on the machine. "And I'm up this late because your cousin came back."

"He's back?" The plate slipped in Grizzy's grip, and the slices teetered dangerously close to the jaws of oblivion—a.k.a. Curly Fries. "Are you serious? This has to be the best night ever. I was so worried about him. Chris, this isn't another one of your weird metaphors I don't get, is it?"

"Weird metaphors? I have no idea what you mean." I took the pizza plate back and put it on the counter instead. Curly could probably reach it, but it would be much easier to cut her off at the pass.

"He's back, Griz. In fact, he made quite the entrance just after you left with Officer Sews His Own Socks."

"That one was lame."

"I can't be on point all the time." I got the coffee mugs out of the cupboard. "He's back, and he's terrified that the cops will think it's him. I managed to squeeze a tiny bit of information out of him too."

"What type of information?" Grizzy asked.

I filled her in on the details, from the supposed art shop theft to Jerry's freak outs then poured us each a mug of the good stuff. We sat at the table in silence and munched on the leftover pizza.

Griz dabbed her lips with a napkin then crumpled it up. "Jerry Lee ran out because he was afraid of being accused. And the real murderer," she said, cutting off to shudder, "was in my house, tampering with the antique hours before Haley's death. Gosh, that gives me all kinds of nasty feelings."

"It gives me one nasty feeling," I said, "the feeling that this was planned out long ago and for a serious reason."

"What do you mean?"

"It's too much of a leap."

"You can tell me, Chris," she said.

I could trust her with anything as long as it didn't actively endanger my life. "I think it's the whole Somerville mafia issue. It's gotten into my head. I keep seeing strings attached to my mother wherever I go."

"What do you mean?"

"Well, the last murder in Sleepy Creek was somewhat messy, desperate, but it was orchestrated. It involved her, right?"

"Right," Grizzy said, and took another sip of coffee.

"I keep wondering if she's involved in this one too. Or if the Somerville Spiders are involved. I'm not suggesting there's a crime ring operating here, but it's suspicious that two murders have occurred in the span of a month. One connected to my mother and the other in a very strange manner."

"Poison is supposed to be the woman's method, isn't it?"

I lifted my coffee mug. "I love a bit of casual sexism with my murder. But no, I can't rule out—"

"Wait a second, what do you mean *you* can't rule out? Christie Lilith Watson, you're not thinking of investigating this murder are you? Need I remind you what happened the last time?" Griz sniffed. "We almost died. And you're lucky Liam didn't decide to put in a call to your Chief back in Boston."

"I'm not investigating, sheesh. I'm just musing is all. Wondering out loud."

"As long as that's all it is," Griz said, but I hadn't done much to alleviate her suspicion. She had her eye on me.

"Oh come on. Jerry came back today and this happened in our friends' antique store. Obviously, I'm going to talk about it."

"I want you to stay safe." Griz patted my hand. She yawned and barely covered it in time. "I want to catch some shut-eye before we open tomorrow. No doubt, we'll have another twisted vine of rumors to wrestle in the morning, all revolving around Jerry Lee. I bet my next-door neighbors saw him arrive."

"Don't worry." I pointed to my mouth and its barbed tongue. "I'm bringing my weed whacker to work tomorrow."

"That's what I was afraid of." Grizzy blew me a kiss and pushed up from the kitchen table. She wandered off. Curly hesitated, sniffed the pizza-free air then followed her.

"Hmmm. Another murder."

It was time I put my thinking cap on.

𝕤 8 𝕤

I was up mystery creek without a paddle. Another case to solve, one I shouldn't get involved in, and one that was definitely more complicated than the last.

It was easy to assume Jerry had been the target of the attack. I couldn't rule out Haley as the intended victim, particularly after what she'd said before her death. Starting with their enemies was the most direct course.

The early morning opening at the Burger Bar hadn't helped clear my thoughts. The restaurant was empty, apart from Jarvis in the kitchen and Martin yawning in the far corner, but I expected the terrible two to make their appearance at 8am sharp.

Griselda hummed under her breath and swayed from side-to-side in front of the mixer.

"Is that—are you singing Britney Spears?"

"It's Joan Jett, actually, and I wasn't singing. I was humming." Grizzy failed to keep a straight face. "I'm sorry. I know I'm terrible. I should be down after what happened yesterday, but last night. Oh my gosh, Christie, last night was magical."

"I'm more concerned by the magical reappearance of your cousin."

"You're right. I'm being over the top. A woman was murdered yesterday, and I'm being selfish, thinking about Arthur Cotton and how much of a gentleman he was." She shook her head. "I'm glad Jerry Lee came back. I'm sure the detectives will be glad too." Her face lit up again—detectives had led her right to thoughts of Arthur.

I couldn't begrudge her the happiness. Griselda's only love had left her for another woman, and she hadn't quite recovered from the sting.

So what if her happiness coincided with a horrifying event?

The front door of the Burger Bar opened, and the terrible twins filed in. Missi had opted for a suit in navy blue, and Virginia had gone with a black maxi dress.

I'd been so focused on why the murder had occurred, I'd written off the cost for these two women. Their store was officially closed until further notice.

Sure, Missi was little rude, but they didn't deserve the loss in business.

"Two Choc Malts?" Grizzy called out.

The pair nodded in unison then shuffled off to their booth against the far wall. Missi didn't even make a beeline for the kitchen to flirt with Jarvis.

Grizzy eyebrows drew in, and she gave me the 'take care of it, Christie' look.

I walked to the table, my tray tucked under one arm. I tilted my head to one side and put up my best 'soft' smile. "How are you ladies holding up?"

"We've been better," Vee said, and snapped open her matching black handbag. She drew out and iPad and placed it on the table. "Any word on the investigation?"

I shifted.

"Oh for heaven's sake, woman. Don't just stand there. Sit down and talk about it properly." Missi drew a tissue from her bag and dabbed beneath her nose.

"Sorry, dear. Mississippi is a little on edge. We've just spoken to Mona Jonah."

"Spoken, pah," Missi said. "She cornered us outside the store and asked us if we were tampering with evidence. The woman is a plague. A yellow-haired, silk-scarfed fopdoodle. I'd like to give her the old one, two."

"You'd break your arms if you tried," Vee replied, sagely, and tapped on the iPad's screen. "But do sit down, dear. It hurts my neck to crane it at you."

"Right." The restaurant was empty, and I *had* planned on chatting to the twins about a possible suspect list anyway.

"This week, please!" Missi clicked her fingers.

At least she'd said 'please.'

Virginia shifted over, and I slid into the booth beside her.

"You're going to investigate it, aren't you?" Virginia asked, without looking up. "Heavens, I can't see a thing on this screen. Did you bring my glasses?"

"No I didn't bring your glasses. Why is everyone fop-doodling around today?" Missi threw up her hands and let them fall into her lap. "Here, you can use mine." She tugged them out of her handbag then foisted them on her sister.

Virginia slipped them on. "Ah, better. It's terrible, this getting old thing."

"I hear age is just a number."

"Tell that to my arthritis," Missi groused.

Virginia prodded me with her bony elbow. "You still haven't answered the question. You're investigating, aren't you?"

"It's not official." Obviously, it wasn't official. It was illegal.

I should've been focusing on my mother's case, but whenever I pictured myself calling up Captain Wilkes to request permission for the case files—yeah, I'd have to get his permission first since I was on sabbatical—my insides turned to sloppy mush.

"That's a yes." Missi dabbed her nose with the tissue again. "And I've got to say, if you didn't do it out of your own initiative, we'd ask you to do it for us."

"What?"

"She's right," Vee put in. "Our store is closed. We had to use the fire escape attached to the upper floor to get out of our apartment today. For the first time in... when was the last time?"

"Never. The last time was never, Virginia,"

Missi replied, then focused on me. "Our store is closed. The Civil War Era artefact has been confiscated as evidence. We're a pariah—"

"Two pariahs. A pair of pariahs?" Virginia suggested.

"Whatever. We're the hot topic for Mona Jonah and her cronies. I won't stand for it, Watson, but there's not a thing I can do about it. I'd like to say I trust Liam to investigate the correct avenues, but he barely saved you from the murderer last time we had one. Besides, I'm not going to leave my fate in the hands of a young man."

I blinked at her. "That's ageist," I said. "And sexist."

"And I don't care."

The pair studied me.

"Look, I don't think you've got anything to worry about when it comes to Detective Balle. From what I've seen, he covers his bases. He does good work. You can trust him."

"Yeah, but he's not a big city cop," Missi said. "He's small town."

"That's not fair," I replied. "He did really well on the last case."

I sounded condescending, but Liam had performed well. He'd put up with my shenanigans.

"Ooh, looks like someone's got a crush on the hunky detective." Vee winked at me. "I don't blame you, dear. He certainly has a swimmer's body."

"Contain yourself, Virginia Waters." Missi shook her head. "Ridiculous. Whatever. He's great. He's a wonderful detective. We still want you to check it out."

"I *may* be invested."

"Got her!" Virginia exclaimed, and the twins high-fived over the table.

"What are you two so excited about?" Griz sidled over with two shakes. She placed one in front of either woman. "I thought you'd be upset after what happened yesterday."

"Oh, it comes and goes." Missi wriggled her nose and gave me a sneaky look. "Say, Griselda, would you tell that darling Jarvis to whip us up two of those delicious Double Cheese Burgers? Please?"

"Of course. Coming right up." Griz hurried off to the counter.

Missi waited until she was out of earshot. "What have you got so far?"

"Nothing much. I have several possible motives. One suspect. An obscure murder weapon, and a window for the setup of the crime which is hair thin. This was obviously premeditated." I drummed my fingertips on the tabletop. "I do need some information from you, actually."

"You do?" Vee looked up from the iPad, blue eyes magnified by the glasses' lenses.

"What do you need?" Missi asked.

"I need a list of Jerry Lee's potential competitors. Antique salesmen, buyers, collectors, preferably folks who've been out of town and to Cleveland in the last month." It was a big ask—it wasn't as if the twins followed their customers or suppliers all over the place, but it was the only hunch I had at the moment.

I couldn't go through Cotton and Balle's files on the murder, or put in a call to a lab and find out more about the poison in that syringe.

"A list," Virginia said. "I could draw something up for you. Email it."

"That would be perfect." I anticipated a late night in front of the TV, eating whatever treat Grizzy baked for a snack, while I researched the potential suspects. I loved that part of the job almost as much as I loved hitting the streets and tracking down the killer.

"William," Missi said, suddenly.

"Pardon me, dear?" Vee adjusted the glasses.

"William Radisson the Third." Missi's vision hazed out.

Jarvis' tinged the bell in the kitchen window. "Order up, mon," he called out. Those burgers, and Grizzy, would be here any second.

"No," Vee said. "He's a snob, but he's not a killer."

"He went to Cleveland a month ago, maybe more. Can't quite remember. But he definitely went to Cleveland. I'm sure of it. And he's extremely competitive. He's the first person you should interview." Missi squeezed her eyes shut for a moment. "There's something else there, but I can't find it. Curse my ancient brain."

"Is there anyone else?" I asked. Grizzy had already collected the tray with its two burger-crammed baskets.

"What about Haley's husband?" Vee put in. "Rich?

"Ah, I didn't know she was married."

"Now you do."

I noted it down, mentally. Spouses were the first on the list of suspects to investigate. Balle would know that too. It might be better to start on the antique suspect list first in that case. The last thing I needed was to head on over to the Combes' residence and run slap bang into Liam.

"Who's that really annoying old lady we don't like?" Missi asked.

"Everyone?" Virginia tapped on the screen and brought it to life. "Ah. Elizabeth. That's her. She queried me about a writing desk last week. I think she might've seen Jerry Lee's website and tried to outbid us for the box."

"Interesting," I said.

"What is?" Grizzy halted beside me.

"Poppies," Missi said. "I was just telling Christie about poppies and how important it is to plant flowers once the threat of frost has passed. Wouldn't want a cold snap to get 'em."

"Poppies?" Griselda's jaw dropped. "Since when are you interesting in gardening, Christie?"

I hated hiding things from my best friend, but she'd lose it if I told her I'd decided to investigate. "Yeah, poppies, totally," I said.

Missi kicked me under the table.

"I mean, I've never had a garden before. I thought it might be fun to keep one."

"Really? I won't say no to that. In fact, I've

got some time this Sunday. We can go down to the Sleeper's Nursery and look for a few plants. Obviously, we can't plant from bulbs right now. It's a little late for that."

I nodded along as if I knew a thing about flowers. "Sounds great. I'll—uh, I'll leave you two to your burgers. The morning rush is due to start pretty soon."

The front door clapped open and two men in overalls entered, right on time. I used their presence as an excuse to slip away before Griselda called my bluff. Heaven knew, she'd figure it out on Sunday in the nursery.

I'd managed to get three names for my list. That was a start.

Something was always better than nothing, right?

9

I unlocked the front door of Grizzy's house at 2pm. I'd opted to hand over my shift to Martin after the twentieth ear-creaking yawn in as many minutes. I would spend the rest of the day tracking down the suspects on the list Missi and Vee had emailed me.

All that cross-questioning and Jerry Lee chatter last night had worn me out. The man himself had gone down to the station this afternoon to have a chat with the detectives, but not before he'd crashed into the Burger Bar in high dramatic panic.

"My life is a soap opera," I sighed.

It was a miracle no one had discovered a long lost brother or sister and gone off in search of a cursed diamond or something.

I let myself into the entrance hall and spotted Curly asleep on the sofa in a circle of sunlight. She didn't meow a greeting, and I gave her the same treatment in return.

The shower called my name. My Burger Bar uniform t-shirt wasn't dirty, per say, but I smelled like the twenty odd Double Cheeses I'd served today.

My phone trilled in the front pocket of my jeans, and I groaned. "So much for that shower." I brought out my device, blinked at the name on the screen, then answered. "Hello. How did you get this number?"

"I have my sources," Virginia replied. Well, that wasn't ominous at all. "Give me a minute. I need to go to the bathroom."

"And you called to tell me?"

"Of course, not. Just wait, dear." A rustle of fabric, muffled footsteps, a slap of a door then silence.

I waited, keys tucked against my palm.

"I can talk," Virginia said.

"Well, that's a relief."

"Cut the sarcasm, dearie. I'm not calling you because I need your help selecting toilet paper."

"No sarcasm this time, but that *is* a relief."

"Oh, you and your smart mouth. I'm glad you have a smart brain to go with it. You need to get over to our place right away. Use the side stairs to get in."

"Why?"

"Because they still haven't unsealed our store," Vee said, then tut-tutted. "It's a shame. We're losing business this way. Thankfully, Missi has come up with an elegant solution."

"No, I mean why do you want me to come over?"

"Missi's been inviting our clients over to

discuss deals. We can't sell at the moment, but we can source antiques and paintings."

"I'm missing something." I scratched my forehead with the front door key.

"William the Third is here," Vee hissed. "And he's practically taken over the living room with his ego. I'm surprised the ceiling hasn't burst at the seams yet. Come over. Pretend you're bringing us food as a form of condolence or support in these trying times."

"If only I had a pie."

"Figure it out, Detective Watson." Vee hung up—she had to be serious if she hadn't even said goodbye. She was anything but rude.

I stowed my phone then tapped my bottom lip. I was tired, and I smelled burgery, but this was the opportunity to have a talk with a suspect. William the Third was connected with the twins, their business, and the antique dealing game.

"Just do it." I bustled through to the kitchen. I slammed open cupboards and rifled through the groceries. A bag of potato chips probably wouldn't suffice. Missi wouldn't let me live it down if I turned up with a jug of OJ either.

"Ha!" I swiped up a bag of cookies. It'd have to do. I'd make some excuse about a broken oven if William the Third had comments about my lack of hospitality.

Fifteen minutes of brisk walking, and I arrived at Terrible Two's Antiques. The front door was taped shut, a police warning to any potential interlopers. I entered the alley down the side of the building then mounted the rickety metal fire escape.

I reached the back door and knocked once, clasping the sweaty bag of cookies to my chest.

The latch clacked and Virginia appeared, her plum colored hair up in a neat bun. "That's the best you could do?" She gestured to the bag.

"Hey, it's something. I'm not the baker in the house."

"Come in, dear." She stepped back, and I

entered their upstairs kitchen. A warm, yellow room filled with the scent of cinnamon apple pie.

"Wow," I said, and swallowed saliva. "Folks in Sleepy Creek sure pull out all the stops." The square kitchen table was piled with containers and casserole dishes.

"The apple pie is from Mona Jonah." Vee shut the kitchen door and locked it too. "We haven't determined whether it's poisoned yet, but we've both decided not to eat it. You can take it if you want."

"I'll pass." They couldn't be serious about the poisoning thing, unless they meant it metaphorically. I didn't doubt Mona's natural toxicity had dripped into the apple filling during the baking process.

"He's in the living room," Virginia said. "Follow me. And try to be—hmm, less cop-like."

Was it that obvious? I followed her through to the next room where I met the suspect. One I could only describe as, well... he kind of looked like Einstein.

Tufty white hair on either side of his head, a matching moustache, and two mellow brown eyes beneath bushy eyebrows. His nose was sharply hooked. He wore a suit, and brought a timepiece from his pocket as I entered. Tarnished timepiece. Not well looked after? Why? All for appearances?

"Goodness, is it that time of the afternoon already?" William the Third goggled at the watch face.

Missi sniffed. "Amazing concept, isn't it? Time passing." Oof, she was in good form today.

"Don't leave yet, William. We haven't discussed our plans for the grand reopening of the store. And our friend here has just brought us some cookies to go with our coffee," Virginia said, and Missi's expression altered—suspicion. Oh yeah, she knew I couldn't have whipped up a batch of choc-chip by myself.

"Cookies," William said. "Splendid." *Another Downton Abbey aficionado. Great.*

"I'm Christie." I walked forward hand outstretched.

He rose from the armchair as I reached him, and I accidently karate chopped the top of his head, right on the bald spot. His skin wrinkled and stayed that way. What on earth?

"Sorry!"

William smoothed fingers over his crown and those tufts of white hair. "That's quite all right. I'm not as spry as I used to be or I'd have been out of the chair before you'd set off." He chuckled then took the handshake. "Charmed. Titillated."

Missi groaned under her breath.

"You must be William," I said. "Virginia has told me so much about you."

"She has?" He hadn't let go of me, and his palm was clammy.

"Of course. You're the best supplier they've ever had."

"Oh well, I won't deny the claim. I do

bring priceless pieces whenever possible. Oh yes, oh my." He waffled on under his breath, and sat back down again, compulsively straightening the faded lapels of his suit.

Everything about William screamed wealth from a distance, but at close range he was somewhat faded.

I backpedaled a few steps and sat down on the plastic covered sofa. It crinkled and squeaked beneath me.

"You mentioned a grand opening?" I asked.

"Oh yes," Virginia said. "We figured we'd take advantage of the upheaval. We're going to get new stock and take out an advertisement in the local paper. And we're going to create a social media page for the store. We're just trying to figure out what we should focus on."

"Paintings, of course," William said. "I can acquire the best and most exclusive artworks for you. I know plenty of art dealers in Ohio."

"You do?" I asked.

"Oh yes, there's a lovely little auction house in Cleveland. I'm friends with a few of the auctioneers."

That much talk equaled little action in my experience. "That's amazing," I said, and fed logs onto the flaming ego.

"Excuse me, I'm going to make us another pot of coffee," Vee said. "Missi, why don't you help me?"

The grump heaved herself off the sofa. "Yes, because that's worthy of two sets of hands." The women exited the room.

I had the suspect all to myself.

"Poor Missi and Virginia," I said, and wrung my hands. "I've been so worried about them. I'm sure you have too."

"Oh?"

"Oh yeah, you know, what happened downstairs." I gave a delicate grimace.

"The death of the girl, yes?" William pursed his lips—the briefest expression of distaste. "Yes, it is terrible for them. They're wonderful old ladies. A little on the lackluster side in the sales department, but oh well."

"What do you mean?"

"They're very selective with their purchases, and I've had less business from them of late. I can't imagine why they'd buy less from a supplier such as myself, but what can I do? Demand calls me elsewhere, anyway. There are many who need my services, and who am I to deny them?"

Somehow my prompt about Haley had been misinterpreted as a plug for his skills as an acquirer of antiques. "You get your wares from Cleveland."

He shuddered at the term 'wares.' "Yes, I'm there every other weekend. Lovely spots."

"You must know Jerry Lee, then," I said.

"Who?"

"Jerry Lee Lewis."

"The singer?"

"No, I—"

The two ladies reentered the living room and cut the conversation short. But, I wasn't too sour about it. I'd done this enough times to know when it wouldn't lead anywhere. William the Third was totally self-involved.

"I was talking to William here about Cleveland and his suppliers. I wondered if he'd run into our friend Jerry Lee before," I said.

"Never heard of him." The man accepted a coffee mug from Vee then took a cookie. He sniffed it and wrinkled his nose. "Is this freshly baked?"

My cheeks heated. "It's a shame what happened to Haley isn't it? She was an artist wasn't she? Did you know her well, William?"

"Not really," the man replied, and took a nibble of the cookie. His lips peeled back in a rictus. "Definitely not freshly baked. I'm afraid I only eat freshly baked." He tossed the cookie back onto the plate on the coffee table and sent crumbs flying. "And I'm afraid I must leave, now, dears. We'll have to talk about antiques for the opening another time. I have a prior engagement, and your home smells like meat."

"What?" Missi's jaw dropped. Apparently, she wasn't used to others providing a dash of rudeness in a social interactions.

"Meat," William replied. "Cooked meat."

I shrank from him. It had to be the Burger Bar's lingering scent.

"I'm vegan." He rose from his seat and shuffled to the exit.

"Here, let me walk you out, William." Virginia set down her coffee mug next to the broken and crumby cookies then followed him.

The old man's waffle drifted off and finally dissipated.

"Vegan, my wrinkled old behind! That man eats more burgers from Grizzy's restaurant than anyone I know," Missi erupted. "He gets them delivered, for Pete's sake. And he definitely knew Haley. He's lying. I hope you've got him on your suspect list."

So, William didn't like the questions, and he'd lied in response to them.

"Everyone's a suspect at this point," I said. "Even you."

Missi snorted and picked up one of the broken cookies. "The only thing suspect in this living room is the store-bought food."

"Gimme a break."

"Only when you've earned it," Missi said, and dipped her sub-par cookie into her mug.

✥ 10 ✥

I rattled down the fire escape, out of range of Missi's vim and vitriole, at least until she stopped by the Burger Bar tomorrow morning. But those were tomorrow's worries. As for now, I had a murder investigation to interfere in.

I took stock.

What had I learned?

That William the Third didn't like cookies from a bag. And that he'd lied to me about knowing Haley. What else had he lied about?

And what was his motivation for dodging the truth?

Something about the man didn't sit right with me. The strange appearances, the attitude, the fake British accent. What did he have to hide?

That's for me to find out.

Right now, I needed to get home, get in the shower, and then get to work. William would be first on my research list. After that would come Haley's husband. I had to find out who he was and exactly where I could find him.

This took top priority—Grizzy's cousin was at risk, after all. Assuming he hadn't done it.

I reached the bottom of Missi and Vee's stairs and set off down the short alleyway between their antique store and the bakery next door to it. The scent of crusty pies and bread and muffins dragged me toward the mouth of the alley.

OK, so maybe I smelled like hamburger

meat and desperately needed a shower, but would it hurt to stop at the bakery first and grab something to go? A croissant would hit the spot right about now. And delicious chocolate dipping sauce. Or...

"We meet again, Mr. Lewis." The uppity British accent traveled from the sidewalk.

I frowned, stepping closer to the mouth of the alley. Those were the snarky tones of William. I peered round the corner and caught sight of him. He stood with his back to me, the hair on the sides of his head shining beneath the afternoon sun.

Jerry Lee was in front of him, his arms folded across his neat checked button down, his ascot rustled by the spring breeze. "Excuse me," he said. "I need to get past."

"To where?" William asked, and it was more of a sneer.

"To go do business that is none of your concern." Jerry's faux British accent was no competition for William's, but it made my head hurt listening to the two of them put it on. It would have been different if either of them had come from the UK. It was the fake part that got to me.

I peeked again, keeping as far back as possible, and witnessed the interaction between the two antique dealers.

Jerry Lee tried stepping past William, and the older man strafed to block him. "I'd be very interested to know what you're doing here of all places."

"It doesn't matter if you're interested. It's still none of your business."

"You're here for them, aren't you? You think you can move in on my turf?"

"It's not your turf, Radisson. We've spoken about this before," Jerry Lee said, and folded his arms. He lifted his chin, but it wobbled slightly. "You won't bully me. I'm not afraid of you."

"You should be, boy. I can buy your whole operation with a single call to my personal banker. Now, I highly suggest you turn around and go back where you came from. Terrible Two's Antiques is my territory now."

Jerry huffed and puffed. "I—I—"

I drew back and walked to the metal staircase that led to the side of the twins' upstairs apartment, then hopped onto it and ran on the spot, clanging my feet as much as possible. I strode down again and around the corner.

William had already sped off down the street, his coat tails flapping. Jerry remained exactly where he'd been moments before.

"Oh hi, Jerry, how are you today? How was speaking to the cops?" I asked, cheerily.

"It was fine. Fine, the ... cops were fine. They asked me questions and I answered them." He looked over his shoulder. "No problems."

"Hey, you look pale. You need to talk about anything?" I took hold of his forearm.

"No, no. I'm OK. I just—"

"I heard what he said, Jerry."

"What?" His gaze snapped up and met

mine. "Oh, William? Oh he was just being ... William."

"Rude was how I would have put it. You two know each other well?" I released him and stepped back, so he wouldn't feel crowded. If Jerry and William knew each other, it was yet another thing William had lied to me about.

"I wouldn't say well," Jerry replied, quickly. "We run into each other from time-to-time, at auctions or sales and so on. Relatively new to the game. He procures antiques and sells them, as well. Mostly to collectors, but it seems he's found Terrible Two's Antiques and wants to claim them for himself."

"But you surely won't let him do that."

"No, I won't." Jerry straightened his ascot. "I most certainly will not. This isn't the first time we've had a bidding war and it won't be the last."

"Bidding for what?"

"Everything from antiques to paintings to jewelry." Jerry Lee shrugged. "It's just part of the business." The color had returned to his face, at last, and he inhaled sharply, then squared his shoulders. "Now, I'm going to head up the stairs for my meeting with the twins."

"You do that." I gave him an encouraging double thumbs up.

"I will." Jerry walked around the corner, and his footsteps sounded on the stairs a moment later.

I set off walking again, taking the long road back to Grizzy's house, opting for Main Street, so I'd get to pass by the Burger Bar and check how things were going there. My mind whirred.

William was a liar and very competitive. But a lot of people were those two things without being murderers. If I wanted to prove anything, I needed evidence, and that was the one thing I didn't have right now.

But how to get it?

The only way was to follow the leads, and I had plenty of them. William, this Elizabeth woman that the twins had mentioned, and then the husband of the victim. All it would take was fancy footwork and avoiding the detectives Cotton and Balle.

I sniggered. I still couldn't get over their names.

"What's so funny?" The voice had come from my left, from the entrance to the second-hand bookstore.

None other than the Detective Balle himself stood in the doorway, grasping a dog-eared paperback in his hand. He held the door open with the other, affording me a brief glimpse of the inside of the store.

I'd been meaning to go in, but life had been too hectic for that the last week.

The shelves behind him creaked beneath their weight in books, and the smell of reading —worn paper and the faintest hint of dusty wood—drifted out.

"Hi," I said.

Balle was in his uniform. He stepped onto the sidewalk and shut the glass door behind himself. It rattled in the jamb. "Hello, Watson. Christie."

"Is that how you're addressing me now? Watson, Christie? I'll call you Balle, Liam, then?"

"Funny."

"I try."

He lifted two fingers and pinched them together. "Maybe you should try a little less." But a smile played around the corners of his lips, and my stomach did a flip.

A flip? What on earth was that about? My stomach did *not* do gymnastics for anyone. Only pizza elicited that level of excitement in me. I cleared my throat. "Doing some lunch time shopping?"

"Kind of," he said, and looked down at his book. "I like to read while I eat."

"Burgers?"

"Maybe. I haven't decided yet."

A passerby squeezed between us, clicking her tongue as she walked. I moved closer to the book store so I'd be out of the way. "What are you reading?" I asked, by way of segue. Maybe, if I could soften him up, I could press him for information about the case?

Balle hid the book behind his back. "Nothing in particular."

"Are you shy?"

"No."

"Then why don't you tell me what you're reading?"

Liam ran his fingers through his dark, shining hair, then brought the book out again. He flashed me the cover.

"The Great Gatsby?" I asked. "That's nothing to be shy about. That's great literature."

"Sure. Guess I'm used to the others at the station taking issue with my reading material. They're more into car magazines. Or gun magazines. Or comics. Not that there's anything wrong with those."

"Well, there's nothing wrong with this, either." Another strange silence started between us.

Our eyes locked. My belly betrayed me again. Were those ... butterflies?

"OK," Balle said, and cleared his throat. "OK, I'd better get going. You have a good day, Wat—Christie."

"Thank you," I said. "I will."

And then he was off, swaggering without trying, his broad shoulders stealing the space on the sidewalk. I stared after him, until, finally a thought occurred to me. I hadn't even squeezed him for information about the case.

What was that about?

I didn't want to dissect that or our odd silences. There was work to be done, and none of it involved mooning over Liam's eyes or shoulders or choice in reading material.

The gossip flowed thick and fast in the Burger Bar the next morning. Folks ate their burgers, slurped down their malt shakes, and cast looks up at the front counter, where Grizzy manned the milkshake bar, and I twirled my tray around on one finger.

I paused to catch it, offering Grizzy a smile. It was mostly to ease her mind—she'd been all over the place the last few days. Firstly, worrying about Jerry Lee, then nervous for her date.

As for me? I already had big plans for the afternoon.

A trip to a certain doctor, who just so happened to be the grieving—though, that was still up for debate—widower of Haley Combes.

"What?" Grizzy asked.

"What?"

"Why are you looking at me like that, Chris?"

"Like what?"

"I don't know ... like Curly when she's about to slurp down a bowl of cream."

"Hmm, I'm not sure what you're talking about," I replied. "But I think we've solved the mystery of Curly Fries' ever-expanding girth."

Grizzy pursed her lips at me. "Cat obesity is no joke."

"Yeah, you're not the one who keeps waking up with Curly asleep on your forehead."

"Talking about your impending doom

again?" Missi appeared and took a seat on one of the barstools. "I'm glad to see you've invested in that cat."

"It's not my cat. It's Grizzy's."

"You have a cat?" Missi asked, and placed a massive tote bag on the countertop in front of her. She clasped her wizened hands over the latch and blinked up at my friend. "When did you get one?"

Griselda gave her a puzzled look. "Years ago. She's always around whenever you've visited, Missi. I can't believe you didn't notice."

"Hmm. I have been distracted."

"For five years?" I asked.

"Don't you start, Watson. I've already got a bone to pick with you."

"You do? Why?"

Missi gestured over her shoulder to the booth she usually sat in with her sister. "Look there."

A happy family was seated in her spot, two children blowing bubbles into their milkshakes and laughing, while their mother scoffed down a burger, and their father read a newspaper. He turned the page and lifted it, showing off its cover.

Murder in Sleepy Creek! Who's Next on the List?

I sighed. That type of title only served to rumor-monger, but then again, with the gossip circle basically in charge of the Creeker Gazette, what did any of us expect?

"I can hardly control who sits where," I said.

"You're the waitress."

"Fair point, but I can't reserve the booth at all hours of the day, you know."

Missi harrumphed, but didn't argue back. Instead, she rapped her knuckles on the countertop. "Can I get a Choc Malt and a burger, please? I want all the good stuff. I need my energy today."

"Coming right up," Griz said, and delivered the order to Jarvis in the kitchen with a ring of the bell.

"Why do you need your energy?" I asked.

"Oh, because we've got another bajillion interviews lined up with potential clients and customers. Collectors who are coming to study the pieces we do have. The whole living room is filled with antiques, some of which I didn't choose, I'll add. I can't even keep track anymore. My ledgers are a mess and that cop of Grizzy's hasn't taken the tape off our store's door yet."

"These things take time," I said. "They have to be thorough with the crime scene."

"Speaking of taking time." Missi leaned in, talking out of the side of her mouth as Griz leaned on the counter in the kitchen window and chatted to Jarvis. "What's going on with your... investigations?"

"Nothing yet. I'll update you when I have something solid. But I do have an appointment with the husband later on," I said.

"Good. Good. Dr. Rich. Piece of work if you ask me. Last month, I went in for a bunion, and he misdiagnosed it as a boil. Ter-

THE DOUBLE CHEESE BURGER MURDER

rible man. I had to get a second opinion from the GP over in Logan's Rest."

"What are we talking about?" Grizzy asked.

Missi and I exchanged a glance. It was difficult to hide the truth from my friend, but it would only upset her. "Flowers," I said. "I was asking Missi what she knew about them. You know, in preparation for our gardening on Sunday."

Before my bestie could reply, or call me out for the lie, the bell above the door tinkled, and she perked up. "Ah, here's Jerry."

We turned in our seats, and there he was. Mr. Lewis with his ascot neat and tidy, a lemon yellow that suited his jaunty disposition. Things had been looking up for him of late. The police hadn't spoken with him or stopped by the house in the past day, and it seemed he'd moved on from the murder.

So easily. Hmmm.

"Good morning," Jerry Lee said, and took a seat on the stool next to mine. He read-

justed his shirt, then placed his leather briefcase on the counter. "Isn't it a wonderful day?"

"It sure is." Grizzy delivered a milkshake
to the counter, and Missi accepted it, then
peeled paper off a straw and inserted it into
the creamy goodness.

She lifted the cherry off the cream and
gobbled it up. "Ah, that's better. The only
thing that puts me in a good mood is one of
your milkshakes, Grizzy. And seeing Jarvis
working hard, of course." She leaned over and
peered at the chef through the kitchen window, grinning.

"I'm in a great mood. I've gotten a lot of
business done, and I know that everything is
going to work out fine," Jerry Lee said.

"What makes you so sure?" I asked, and
twirled the tray again. "Did they say something to you?"

"Well, no," Jerry said, and placed a hand on
the top of his briefcase. "But I know I'm innocent, and that means they can't arrest me for
something I didn't do. I trust the justice

system."

"That's the spirit," Grizzy said. "What can I get for you, Jerry?"

"Oh, how about one of your specials?"

"Sure, I can do that."

"But hold the onions, please."

"No pro—" Grizzy cut off.

"No pro?" I asked.

But she shook her head.

I glanced in the mirror behind the bar and caught sight of what had freaked her out. The two detectives had entered the restaurant. No one paid them any mind—it wasn't unusual to spot the local cops in the Burger Bar. This place did have the best burgers in town. But the look on Balle's face told me he wasn't here for a Double Cheese.

The officers strode between the tables and came to a halt at the bar next to me. Detective Balle's woody cologne drifted over, and I forced myself not to react.

"Good morning," Grizzy said, and offered

Arthur a nervous smile. "What can I get for you gentleman today?"

"Nothing, Miss Lewis," Balle replied. "We're here for Jerry Lee."

Arthur nodded, though he wouldn't quite meet Grizzy's eye.

"Of course," Jerry Lee said, jovially. "What can I help you with?"

"I'm afraid you're going to have to come with us, Mr. Lewis." And Balle drew a set of cuffs from his belt.

Griselda went pale and pressed her hands to her cheeks.

I groaned and put my tray down. "Really? You're going to do this here?"

"We have a warrant from the judge for your arrest, Mr. Lewis," Balle said, ignoring me completely. "I'm going to ask you to come with us, peacefully, and I won't have to put these cuffs on you. Will you comply?"

Jerry trembled on the spot, the confidence draining from him, immediately. "But I'm inno-

cent. You have to know I'm innocent. I didn't'
do anything wrong!" The last bit came out too
loud, and the other diners in the Burger Bar
turned their heads, lowered their voices.

"Will you comply?" Balle repeated.

"Don't make this any harder than it has to
be, Jerry Lee," I said. "Go with them. They'll
take you either way."

Jerry glanced from me to Balle then back
again. Finally, he got off the chair. "All right.
I'm coming."

Arthur stepped up to Jerry's side. Balle
took a position on the other. Together the
men walked him toward the door. Balle's voice
was hushed, but it traveled in the now quiet
restaurant. "You have the right to remain
silent. Anything you say can and will be used
against you in a court of law. You have the
right to an attorney..."

The door opened, and the men exited
onto the street. Jerry Lee was guided toward
the cruiser parked out front.

"This isn't happening," Grizzy said. "How can they do that?"

"They have a warrant. They're well within their rights."

"But how? Jerry Lee's innocent."

The cruiser drove off, and the talk in the restaurant resumed, folks leaning forward to discuss what had happened with renewed fervor. This would be the talk of Sleepy Creek for the next week. Until someone had an affair or Maura's cat started another turf war.

"They have reason to believe he committed the crime," I said.

"But—"

"Griz, the police can't make an arrest like that unless they have evidence that indicates he was involved in the murder," I replied.

"He's not." Grizzy folded her arms.

Missi slurped on her milkshake, her eyes shifting back and forth, observing us.

"They think he is."

"But ... look, there's got to be a way to help him. I know my cousin wouldn't hurt

THE DOUBLE CHEESE BURGER MURDER

anyone. He certainly wouldn't *murder* them. He's innocent. I'll prove it. Somehow. I don't know how."

"I think I know how," Missi said.

"How?"

"Ask Christie to help. She's a detective, and she might be able to solve the case. If she thinks Jerry Lee is innocent, then maybe she can find out who really did it and clear his name."

I met Missi's gaze, briefly. If this got me out of the Sunday poppy planting escapade, then I was all for it. That and I wasn't entirely sure Jerry had done it. He was still on the suspect list, but I didn't have any evidence to support the assumption.

If only I had access to what Balle does. To the files.

"I couldn't ask her to do that," Griz said. "That would endanger her career back in Boston."

"I'm happy to help. Let's face it, Griz, this is what I do best, and I'm not going to sit back when the murder happened so close to home. It's affected Missi and Vee, it's affecting you and your family too."

Griz licked her lips. "It would be selfish of me to say yes after I've been so set on you not doing exactly that."

"Let's put it this way," I said, and pressed my palm to the countertop. "I'm already looking into it, and I'm going to continue." It felt good to get the truth off my chest.

"You are?" Before Griz could reprimand me, Jarvis dinged the bell in the kitchen window.

"Order up, mon."

My bestie collected the burger in its basket and delivered it to Missi. "You're sure about this, Chris?"

"Sure as I've been about anything," I replied.

"Well, if you're doing it, then I'm going to help you."

"What? No way. You can't—"

"I'm helping." Grizzy's bottom jaw jutted out. "Just try to stop me."

One of the customers at the table's raised a hand, and I collected my tray and hurried off before Griz could get into her stride. She'd made up her mind, and I respected that. How could I fault her for wanting to help her friends when I was doing exactly the same?

I halted next to the table and put up my best customer-related smile. "What can I get for you, ma'am?"

She rattled off an order, and I took it down, hoping I'd gotten it right. My mind was already fixated on today's investigations and freeing Jerry Lee.

If he deserves to be freed.

🌿 I 2 🌿

"**A**re you sure you want to do this?" I asked, as I slipped off my apron in the Burger Bar.

The lunch rush had ended, and the tables had emptied out in the interim. Those who still lingered sipped coffees and read on their Kindles or out of paperbacks. Martin, the other waiter, stood in the corner, his gaze sweeping over the restaurant. He was a far better waiter than I could ever be—attentive, definite manager material.

"Yes, I'm sure," Grizzy said. "I'm coming

with you. I need to get used to doing things that put me out of my comfort zone. Besides, Martin will take care of the place while I'm gone, and it's nowhere near the dinner rush."

"If you say so." We left the Burger Bar and moved into the sunshine on the sidewalk. Cars drove by at their leisure, and folks who weren't in their stores, manning the front desks, walked down the street window shopping or stopping to chat with other residents.

A bus pulled up next to a stop, its doors snapping open to accept passengers headed out of Sleepy Creek and letting others off. That had been me a short while ago—funny, it felt like years had passed since that day.

"So," Grizzy said, as she joined me, "what time is your appointment with Dr. Rich?"

"In about a half hour," I replied.

"Good, that gives me more than enough time."

"Time for what?"

"To get a leash on Curly Fries, of course. She needs her walk."

I blinked at my friend. "Her walk?"

"Yes, of course."

"Griz, we're going to interview a doctor about his dead wife," I whispered. "I don't think bringing Curly along is appropriate."

"Weren't you the one who pointed out how fat she's getting?"

"Yes, but—"

"And isn't it true that she should walk more if she wants to lose weight?"

"Yes, but that's hardly—"

Griz raised her index finger. "And isn't it true that we're not even supposed to be asking questions and the fact that we are is, in itself, pretty inappropriate?"

I cleared my throat.

"Exactly. Bringing Curly along doesn't make a difference."

"Fine. But I'm not happy about it. If she steps on my toes, she's never coming on another trip with me again." I meant that both literally and figuratively.

"You don't have the authority to make that

call, unfortunately." Grizzy gave me a cheeky grin as we set off down Main Street, heading toward suburbia. The sights and sounds of the town surrounded us, and I let the warm atmosphere wash over me. It was the way of Sleepy Creek.

Secrets, yes, but the hospitality was there too. People smiled and waved at us, even though a murder had happened only a few days prior. They cared around here, and it was a nice change of pace after living in the city for such a long time.

That wasn't to say people in the city didn't care, it just wasn't at this level.

You're not getting soft are you? Remember, this is a vacation.

We reached Grizzy's double story with its brick face and sash windows, and I waited outside while she darted in to get the cat on a leash. I tapped my foot, studying the neighborhood, from the high fences that separated Ray Tolentino's place from Grizzy, to the gorgeous maple tree in her front yard.

The door slammed, and Griz reappeared with Curly on the end of a leash. It was pink and glittery, and her collar matched it. Curly looked about as disgusted by the whole affair as I was, her black fur practically standing on end.

"All right. Let's go," Grizzy said, cheerily.

We set off for the doctor's office at a glacial pace, and I checked my watch intermittently, clicking my tongue at Curly Fries. She waddled along, her tail straight as a poker, and ignored my prompting.

At last, we made it to Dr. Rich's practice and let ourselves inside.

The receptionist, Patricia, gave us a welcoming smile. "Good morning, how may I help you?"

"Hi. I have an appointment with Dr. Rich? For... now, actually."

"Your name?"

"Christie Watson."

"Take a seat, the doctor will be with you shortly."

I thanked her and we retreated to the set of taupe sofas against the wall. There was a selection of magazines that ranged back into the 90s on the table, and a water cooler in the corner with Styrofoam cups.

"What's the procedure for this?" Grizzy drew Curly into her lap. "The interview, I mean."

"I'll do the talking, you just give him either menacing or kind looks, depending on how it's going. Think of this like … your first day on the job. You watch what I do."

"Oh, like I'm shadowing you?"

"Exactly."

The door to the doctor's room opened, and a man appeared. He was middle-aged, tall. Blocky head, but compulsively neat—the collar of his shirt was stiff, his hair brushed to one side, the tracks the comb's bristles had made still visible.

"Miss Watson?" He beckoned to me.

I got up and led the way into the office itself, noting the degrees he'd hung up on his wall. There were no family pictures, save for the frame on his desk which faced the other way.

"Please, take a seat." Dr. Rich lowered himself into his executive leather chair. "What can I help you with today?" His gaze traveled to Griz and Curly, who had taken a spot in one of the chairs in front of his desk. "I'm afraid I can't treat animals. There is a veterinarian I can recommend, though, if that's what you're looking for."

"No," I said.

"Oh. Oh, all right. Then—"

"We're friends of Haley's," I said.

The doctor's face fell, immediately. He lowered his head and rustled papers on his desk.

"We wanted to offer our condolences for your loss," Grizzy put in. Curly meowed on her lap and tried leaping off. She caught her and held her fast. "We're so sorry. Haley went to high school with us. She was a lovely person."

Up for debate, but whatever.

"Thank you," Dr. Rich said. "But if that's all, I'm—"

"That's not all," I replied. "I don't know if you're aware, Dr. Rich, but I'm a detective."

"I've already spoken to the Sleepy Creek PD."

"Of course," I said, "but I'm investigating this case in my personal capacity. Consider it a citizen's investigation."

"Is that legal?" Rich asked, and smoothed his already neat hair.

"It's frowned upon."

"But not illegal?"

"The point is," I said, "that we can help you. We knew Haley. We know a lot of the people in Sleepy Creek."

"So do the police."

I was at a loss here. I really wasn't the best with dealing with people.

"Sure, but we just want to make sure that whoever did this is brought to justice," Grizzy put in. "This is our town, after all, Rich. I mean, you wouldn't like to see someone else get hurt, I'm sure, and neither would we. We Creekers need to stick together. I know that Haley would have appreciated us helping out. We were there." Curly gave another meow and writhed in Grizzy's grip. "When it happened."

"You were?" Rich asked.

"Yeah," I said. "We were. I witnessed it firsthand. You can imagine that's left a bit of a scar on me. I just want to get to the bottom of it, so it's laid to rest. You know?" It was the emotional tack—I wasn't great with that either.

Rich was silent for a while, his eyebrows drawing inward over a hazel gaze. He reminded me of an owl. A somewhat handsome, potentially murderous owl.

Rich here, would have had ample access to free syringes.

Then again, it was just as easy to buy syringes at the drug store.

"All right," Rich said. "I understand. What do you want to know?"

I scooched to the edge of my chair. "Do you know anyone who might have wanted to hurt Haley?"

"No," Rich said. "Haley had her bad moments, like any of us do, but she wasn't mean, and she didn't make enemies. She was loved by everyone, including me."

Why did he think it was necessary to say that? He's her husband, of course he loves her.

"And has anything strange happened of late? Did Haley tell you about any confrontations or accidents? Any stalking incidents, perhaps?"

"No. Well ... wait, see she spent a lot of her time painting, even during the evenings, so we didn't talk too much about her clients or what she got up to in the day. I've got my work too. Always busy." He ended off with a belated and out of place chuckle. "But—um, there was one thing."

"What?"

"We had a break-in a while ago," he said. "At the house? Both of us were out at the time. It was strange because not much was taken other than Haley's costume jewelry."

"When did that happen?" I asked, tempted to whip out a notepad and start taking jotting things down, but I'd left it back in my apron at the diner.

"About two or three weeks ago? I can't recall the exact date."

"Did you report it to the police?"

"No, no, nothing was broken and it was just some costume jewelry." Rich broke eye contact. "There's not much more I can tell you. Haley was loved. That's all I can say."

A break-in that wasn't reported and nothing else.

Curly meowed a third time and leaped free of Grizzy's lap. She pounced onto the desk and scrabbled across it, making directly for Rich. His eyes widened, and he cried out, lifting his hands.

But Curly had already honed in on her target. Her tail whapped against the picture frame on the desk, and it fell to the carpet

with a thump. The cat hopped into the doctor's lap and scratched at his top pocket.

"Curly!" Grizzy yelped.

"Get it off me." Rich pushed his hands
onto Curly's head, trying to fend her off.

The cat was unrelenting—she growled and
meowed and clawed his shirt, hooking herself
into the fabric.

Griselda hurried around to the doctor's
side of the desk and grabbed her from his lap.
Her claws stuck fast in the cotton, and Grizzy
had to unhook them one-by-one before she
finally got the animal free.

"What on earth was that about?" she
asked, backing up while Curly meowed, her
pupils taking up most of her eyes. "I'm so
sorry, doctor. I don't know why she did that."

"Have you got something in your pocket?"

Dr. Rich brought out a semi-squashed
piece of string-cheese, still in its plastic. "I
was saving it for later."

That settled it. Curly definitely had an ad-
dictive personality type.

"I'm so so sorry," Grizzy said, as Curly went mad yet again, flipping this way and that in her grip. "I'll get her out of here."

The door clicked shut behind the mad cat and her carrier, and I gave the doctor a sheepish grin. "Sorry about that."

"It's all right." But Rich looked dazed after the encounter.

"I'll give you some space." I got up, and my foot nudged the picture frame. It was face up on the carpet. "Oh." I bent and lifted it, studying the image behind the glass.

Rich stood between two women. Haley was on his left, her smile radiant, her skin glowing, and another woman was on his right. She was so old she was almost decrepit—her skin looked paper thin.

"Is this your mother?" I asked.

"No." Rich snatched the picture frame from my grasp. "That's Elizabeth. She's a friend of the family and one of Haley's clients. Now, if you'll excuse me..."

"Of course. Of course." I walked to the

door. "Sorry again. We couldn't have anticipated she'd go crazy like that. The cat."

"Yes. That's fine. Good afternoon." Rich
held the picture in one hand, tilting it toward
himself so the image was shielded from my
view.

I nodded and slipped out of his office,
shutting the door.

*Elizabeth. Was that the same Elizabeth on the
list Missi and Vee sent me?*

There was only one way to find out.

I brought my phone out of my pocket and
made the call.

❧ 13 ❧

After the disaster that was Curly Fries, there was no debate in my mind that she had to stay home during my future investigations. Who knew what smell might trigger another attack on a doctor or innocent passerby?

Besides, it was much easier to focus on snooping when I didn't have a chunky cat waddling around ahead of me or Grizzy cooing at her every five seconds.

And I wasn't ready to give up on my line of questioning yet.

I double-checked the location Virginia had sent to my cellphone from her iPad and followed the GPS directions. The long orange line on my screen led through the center of Sleepy Creek, down Main Road, onto Fletcher Street, then took several twists and turns, right into the heart of 'Money Bags Town.'

That was what most of the citizens of Sleepy Creek called the area where a lot of its wealthier residents stayed.

There were five mansions in total in 'Money Bags Town,' and the one furthest from its heart, and thus, from Sleepy Creek, belonged to a one Elizabeth Wortley. The ancient woman had employed Haley, and Dr. Rich clearly didn't want me to know about.

My legs burned from the walk, but shoot, it was better for the environment, and it helped me burn some calories from the burgers.

I'd broken my 'no burgers at work' rule multiple times this week. And then there'd been the pizza. If I didn't watch out, I'd start looking like Curly Fries and clawing people's pockets for cheese.

The sun was low in the afternoon sky. I'd have a long walk back in the dark if I wasn't quick about this. I entered the 'Money Bags' area of town and strode down the long wide road that wound between the mansions.

Most of them were far removed from the street, presenting their bronze or silver gates as a front. Finally, I reached the last one. The gates here bore a decorative *EW* and shimmered gold.

I hit the button for the intercom and waited.

A camera above the gate swiveled toward me.

"Who's that?" A woman's voice.

"Hi," I said. "Hi there. I'm Christie Watson? I'm a friend of ... of Haley's. I was hoping to talk to you?"

"Talk to me? About what?"

"About Haley. I know that she worked for you. She was a friend of mine, kind of. I wanted to figure out what happened to her and if you might know something." It was the best excuse I could come up with, and, frankly, that was pretty sad. But I was banking on this woman having liked the victim and wanting to talk about her.

"Are you with the police?"

"Not technically ma'am. Not in a professional capacity."

Another pause. The camera's lens extended.

The gates lurched then opened on electric rails, affording me entrance to the long winding road that led between trees.

I took the opening as an invitation.

It was beautiful here, the trees brushed gently by the spring breeze, and the scent of flowers reached my nose as I turned the curve in the road and entered the garden. Exquisitely kept, there were flowerbeds and statues and a central fountain that depicted a woman in a flowing dress, pouring water from a vase.

The mansion, beyond all the prettiness,

was a triple story home with columns on the front porch. The grand doors swung open, and a woman emerged from within, a cane clasped tightly in one hand.

Elizabeth Wortley was even more ancient close up, her skin nearly translucent with age, and her eyes rheumy, but she bore a bright smile that lit up her face. "Hello there, dear. You must be, Christie. My assistant tells me you want to talk about dear Haley."

"I do."

"Come in, come in." She gestured with her cane. "I'll have some coffee and snacks brought into the living room. Isabella! Isabella, darling, bring us something to eat, will you?" She called the last bit as she entered the mansion.

The place was all hardwood and red carpeting and glittering chandeliers. It blurred past as Elizabeth led me into her living room and sat me down on a cream chaise lounge. She took a seat in an armchair across from me, her wrinkled hands clutching the golden head of the walking stick.

"It's good to see you, Miss Watson. I've been watching your progress with great interest."

"Pardon me?"

She smiled again and even her wrinkles had dimples. "You're new to this town, yes? A homicide detective from Boston."

"How do you know that?"

"I have my sources."

"Which sources?"

"Well, they're private. Where would be the fun in revealing them?" Elizabeth chuckled. "Don't worry, dear, I'm not going to report you to the police. That handsome Detective Balle wouldn't appreciate your presence here, I'm sure."

"What do you mean?"

"Oh, dear, I think you know what I mean. All your investigations? News travels fast in this town and through my sources too." Elizabeth leaned in. "Don't worry, dear, I'm an admirer of your work."

"My work?"

"Your investigations," she said. "And I do want to help you clear this horrible matter up. Poor Haley. She was such a lovely girl and a talented artist as well. I miss her dearly."

A maid entered, dressed in an apron and carrying a tray, she had a sharp hooked nose that reminded me of... something. I couldn't make out what. She placed the tray on the coffee table, then unpacked two mugs of steaming coffee, sugar, creamer, and a small tiered cake display bearing miniature donuts.

"Ah, perfect, Isabella, thank you."

The woman dipped into a curtsy—an actual curtsy—and lingered a moment. Her gaze met mine, and a quick smile flashed across her lips. Finally, she turned and left the room.

Odd.

"Please, help yourself." Elizabeth gestured toward the treats.

I was a little freaked, if I was honest. She

knew a lot and had let me in. *Like a spider luring in a fly? What does she really want?*

"Thank you," I said.

Elizabeth removed the coffee from the table and drank her mug black, licking her lips appreciatively. "I love coffee. So strong and invigorating. This is a special bean from Colombia. Try it."

I picked up my coffee and took a sip. "Fragrant."

"Isn't it?"

My nerves built. It didn't taste like poison, but then, who knew? *Now, you're being paranoid.*

"So," Elizabeth said, and placed her coffee back on the table. "What do you want to know about Haley? Or about me? Am I suspect in your investigation? Oh, how exciting!"

"Not the adjective I would have chosen," I replied.

"Ha, you *are* funny."

I put my coffee down too, trying to regain clarity in this situation. I'd been expecting resistance, at least, but this Elizabeth seemed itching to help. And it didn't exactly set me at ease.

It was suspicious. Why would she want to help me? And why had she been listening out for my movements?

"Dear? Do you have questions?" Elizabeth lifted a plate and placed a miniature donut on it, then dusted her sugary fingers off over it. "About Haley?"

"How did you meet Haley?"

"I have a certain compulsion when it comes to antiques. I'm a collector, and Haley was a fantastic artist. She recreated several pieces that I couldn't acquire. Paintings, see? And she had an ear for the best deals. In fact, she started dealing antiques to me. Everything from teapots to jewelry to antique chairs. She was savvy with that internet stuff, whereas, I was totally inept. She became ... close to me. A true friend."

"I see. And would you say she had any enemies?"

"No, no, of course not. Haley was lovely.

Her husband, Rich? He's the doctor in town, and he's great too. A real man." Elizabeth sighed. "I don't know who in their right mind would want to hurt her. Although..."

"What?"

"I did notice her behavior had changed over the past week or two. She mentioned someone had broken into her home. Nothing important had been taken, apart from one of her rings, but she was upset about it. And then—" Elizabeth took a bite of her donut and chewed pensively.

I tapped my foot and absently took a sip of my coffee.

"About three days before her ... her death, Haley was here, helping me select a few antiques from online stores. She received a call on her cellphone. She answered it and left the room, but I heard her arguing with someone. I couldn't make out what was being said, but she sounded irate. And when she came back in, she had tears in her eyes. Very concerning." Another bite of the donut came after that.

"Did she say who it was on the other end of the line?" I asked.

"No, she wouldn't talk about it. When I asked, she tried to pretend it hadn't happened. She wanted to continue with our day as usual."

So, Haley had had a disagreement with someone. And she'd been robbed. Clearly, she was a target—and if she was the intended target, that ruled out Jerry Lee.

"Is there anything else you can tell me about Haley? Anything you think would be relevant?"

"No, that's about it. She was a happy young lady most of the time."

She hadn't seemed it in the store. She'd been grumpy and rude. Was that a clue in itself?

"And what about the other folks in the town?" I asked.

"Which folks?"

"Just off the top of my head, Jerry Lee Lewis?"

"The singer?"

"No, the antique salesman."

"I'm afraid I don't know him," Elizabeth said, and took another bite of her donut. "But the antique game in this town is very ... exciting. People are serious about their collections, as am I. That's why I first contracted Haley to work for me. See, she was affordable and knowledgeable too."

"Affordable?"

"Why, yes. Don't let appearances fool you, dear. This is my ancestral manor, but I'm by no means, rolling in the dough, as you young-ones might put it."

"I see. I'm sorry for imposing."

"Oh, no, no. It's no imposition. Is there anyone else you wanted to know about? I do have my ear to the ground, as I'm sure you've surmised."

"What about William Radisson?"

"The third?"

"That's the one," I said.

"Oh, he's a friend of mine. I met him about four months ago at one of the auctions.

Wonderful man. Comes for coffee and treats on occasion. If I was spryer, I'd spend more time attending auctions with him, but unfortunately, that can't be."

A thought cropped up, and I licked my lips. "So, who did you send to the auctions instead of you? If you can't go, I mean."

"Oh, well, I used to send dear Haley, sometimes my assistant, Isabella. Mostly, he would come here to sell me his wares."

"And you'd say he was nice to you?"

"Of course. Standup guy. Why wouldn't he be nice?"

I didn't have an answer for that. And I was out of questions. I placed my coffee mug on the table, then rose. "Well, thank you for your time, Mrs. Wortley."

"It's Ms."

"Ms. Wortley. I'd better get going before the sun sets."

"You should let my chauffer take you home."

Because that would look normal—me driving home in some fancy limousine. "No, that's all right. Walking gives me time to think. Thank you for your time and your hospitality." And the extra set of suspicions.

"No problem at all, dear."

I nodded then walked for the exit.

"Oh, and Miss Watson," she called.

I looked back over my shoulder at the old woman, seated on her chair like it was a throne, her half-eaten donut sitting on a fine China plate. "Good luck with your investigation. Be careful out there."

❧ 14 ❧

The mood in the Burger Bar the morning after Jerry Lee's arrest was... unique.

Grizzy was down about what had happened, but determined to save her cousin from the hands of the law. She was convinced he was innocent. I wasn't just yet. I had a list of suspects that was too long, especially, after my encounter with Elizabeth the evening before, and Jerry was still on it.

Whatever the case, Haley had had an enemy—petty theft did happen in Sleepy

Creek on occasion, but a break-in for some costume jewelry? It didn't add up.

"Order up, mon." Jarvis dinged the bell in the kitchen window, and I hurried around the side of the bar and collected a burger in a basket with a side of skinny fries.

"Thank you, Jarvis."

"My pleasure." Jarvis flashed a toothy smile.

He was the one constant in the diner that never faltered. Always cheerful and cooking the best burgers around, sometimes humming under his breath. It was difficult to be down with him here.

I carried the burger out to a table in the corner and delivered it to the waiting woman —Nelly Boggs, from the florists'.

"Thank you so much," she said. "I'm starving. You wouldn't believe the morning I've had." Nelly always had a kind word. She was a mousy young woman, brown hair and thick spectacles. She'd caught a leaf in her hair.

"Busy at the florists'?"

"Yeah." Nelly took a sip of her soda. "Everyone's buying flowers for the funeral this weekend. Haley."

"Of course." I nodded.

"And they're all gossiping too." Nelly pulled a face. "About poor Grizzy's cousin. They want to know what's going on. I understand that everyone's afraid or intrigued, and that Sleepy Creek is gossip orientated. I grew up here, but still. Disrespectful. I wish they were more focused on poor Haley than they were on Jerry Lee."

"That's the nature of the town, unfortunately."

Nelly gave a glum nod.

"Enjoy your meal!" I headed for the counter again. The morning rush had already ended, but I was pooped from it. I lowered myself onto the stool in front of the bar and gave Grizzy a thumbs up.

"What a day," she said. "I swear, people *just* want to talk about Jerry. I've had about ten people come in and ask me about it this morning. It's exhausting."

"Sorry, Griz."

"It's OK. It's not your fault. I just wish I understood why they had arrested him. He did nothing wrong, I would bet my life on it."

"Don't do that," I said. "That's a risky thing to say in Sleepy Creek nowadays."

Griz sighed. "Want a milkshake? I'm in the mood for a double thick."

"Flavor?"

"Chocolate for me."

"I'll take a caramel."

"Good choice." Grizzy busied herself making the milkshakes, while I turned on my stool, balancing my elbows on the counters and studying the tables, in case any of them needed anything.

In the week since I'd started here, I'd grown used to the ins and outs of being a waitress. It wasn't as easy as I'd hoped. Not only did I have to be friendly and outgoing, make conversation

with people—which I definitely wasn't used to
—but I had to manage the orders, collect the
money and do everything in between.

The bell over the door rang, merrily, and a
familiar figure entered the restaurant. Yellow
hair, violently red shade of lipstick, and a
leopard print scarf wrapped around her neck.

Mona Jonah.

I half-expected a murder of crows to appear overhead at the mere thought of her
name.

The gossip monger had returned, her magnificent tote slung over one forearm. She waddled over to the bar and set it down on one of
the vinyl topped stools. "Well, hello there,
Griselda." She gave a triumphant smile. "Watson." She didn't even look my way.

"Jonah," I replied, through gritted teeth.

She definitely hadn't come to spread cheer
and good will—she did look a little like a small
town Mrs. Claus to be fair. Mona seated her
behind on another stool and rested her bejew-
eled fingers on the countertop. "I'll take a

milkshake, Griselda," she said, "since you're already making them."

"Which flavor, Mona?" Grizzy asked, in a put-on cheerful voice.

"I'll take a strawberry." Those cougar-length fingernails went tappity-tap-tap.

"So, what brings you in here, Mona?" I asked, casually. "You usually don't come in for a strawberry shake unless you're looking to cause trouble."

"Cause trouble?" Mona raised an eyebrow. "No, dear, if I wanted to cause trouble I would have ordered the vanilla, just for the irony. I'm on a quick break from behind the counter, so I thought I'd grabbing something sweet and fulfilling."

"The counter?" I asked.

"Mona works at the drug store."

"Oh, and here I was thinking you were the editor of the Creeker Gazette."

"Co-editor," the other woman replied. "And only in my spare time."

Grizzy delivered the three milkshakes, one

for her, for me, and for Mona, then took a sip, shutting her eyes as she drank it down.

"Delicious," I said.

Mona's lip curled as she poked her straw into the thick milkshake.

I turned my head, studying Mona. "Say," I said, "you must hear a lot of gossip in the drug store."

"Excuse me?"

"I'm not insulting you. I'm making an observation. I bet," I continued, hoping this ploy would work, "I bet that you could be helpful in an investigation. Have the police even spoken to you about what happened?"

"No," Mona replied, bitterly. "They haven't because they don't know what's good for them."

I took another sip of my milkshake and glanced at my tables—no one needed my help yet. "What do you think of this whole thing?"

"It's pretty obvious what I think. The man who did it is currently in custody." She flashed Grizzy a smile. "He's an outsider, he ran out on the scene of the crime, and the police clearly have enough evidence to hold him, otherwise he would have been out by now. Wouldn't he, dear?"

Griz didn't answer.

This wasn't the line of questioning I'd intended to pursue. "But you haven't seen any real evidence of that," I replied. "I mean, he hasn't bought a syringe from the drugstore."

"No one has, that I know of." Mona waved. "It's all irrelevant, now."

Nelly raised a hand at her table, and I made to get up.

"Let me go," Grizzy said. "I need to keep myself busy." She swept off toward the table and left me with the meanie of the hour. Or the town. Both suited Jonah just fine.

"You're having fun teasing Grizzy," I said. "You should be careful."

"Why?" Mona asked, the straw between her teeth. "Is she going to set her cousin on me?"

"Very funny, Mona. Very funny. But it

hasn't been proven that Jerry is guilty yet, so there is the chance that the murderer is somewhere in Sleepy Creek. The more trouble you cause, the more attention you draw to yourself..." I left her to make the deductions.

"Is that a threat?" Mona asked.

"Of course not. Like I said, it's an observation. That's what I do."

Mona pursed her lips and continued drinking her shake, trying to ignore me now.

"You know, it's a pity."

"What is?" she asked.

"When you came in, I was hoping to talk to you about the murder in an unbiased fashion. I was so sure that you'd be able to help me figure out the missing link, but, oh well, guess you don't know as much as I thought you did." I finished off my milkshake in record time—couldn't help myself with Grizzy's shakes—then walked the glass to the kitchen.

"Wait," Mona said. "What do you mean? What missing link?"

"Hmm, I heard a rumor that I'm not sure

is true." I had to play this just right. Give Mona enough intrigue to keep her guessing. She clearly fed off this type of thing.

And indeed, the woman sat stiff as a stick on her stool, focused on me, the milkshake forgotten. "What rumor?"

I sat down next to her and leaned in, lowering my voice to a whisper. "I heard that Haley's house was broken into, and that she'd been arguing with someone on the phone right before it happened." It went against every bone in my body to share that information, but I needed insight into Haley's personal relationships, and who better to ask than the chief of the Gossip Circle?

"Really?" Mona licked milkshake off her lips.

"You didn't hear that?"

"No. Must be a best kept secret, but I bet I know who she was arguing with," Mona said.

"Who?"

"Isn't it obvious? Her husband. Everyone

knows they were on the brink of getting a divorce when Haley died."

"They were?" It was news to me. Both Elizabeth and Rich had indicated that the couple were happy or I'd have flagged it, right away.

"Of course. There were rumors, you know, that Rich was having an affair, and that Haley had discovered it. It's a miracle that the police didn't arrest him first, but then, I suppose they have their reasons."

That and they can't arrest anyone they want. "News to me," I said, and tapped my chin. "Interesting."

"Yes, Maura told me that she saw Rich with another woman not one week before Haley's death. Apparently, she couldn't see who it was, but they drove off together in an SUV in the late evening."

"When was this?"

"I'm not sure on the exact day. All I can say is it wasn't entirely a surprise. Haley wasn't the most affectionate person around, and, from what I heard, she was having an affair herself with someone in Cleveland."

I stared at Mona, but my brain had clicked on like a cartoon lightbulb. "Cleveland?"

"Yeah." Mona scooched back and forth on her barstool, preparing for the next bit of juicy gossip. "Haley traveled a lot for work. She would go to auctions to buy antiques or artwork, and rumor had it that she was having an affair with one of the auctioneers. Or the bidders. I'm a bit fuzzy on the details, but the rumors are there." Mona smacked her lips. "If I'd have guess who'd done it before Jerry Lee was arrested, I would have said Rich. He was clearly unhappy, and she didn't want to sign the divorce papers so..."

Griselda appeared with a basket in hand and carried it into the kitchen, through the swinging doors.

Mona focused on her milkshake again. The dull slurps of her drinking it was the backdrop to the endless questions now spinning through my mind.

Haley having an affair with someone in Cleveland? Was it hearsay or truth? I couldn't prove it now without finding out for myself. But that wouldn't be easy given that she was gone.

And Rich had cheated on her too?

Now, there was something I could check out. If Rich had something to hide, he clearly did since he hadn't mentioned any of this to us the other day, I'd get to the bottom of it.

A crash rang out from the kitchen, and Grizzy let out a squeal.

"Good heavens," Mona said. "What a rowdy restaurant.

"I'm OK." Griselda appeared in the kitchen doorways, grinning, and her cheeks as shiny red as candy apples. "I'm OK. Say, Chris, could you help me in here for a second?"

The investigation would have to wait until tonight.

🦋 15 🦋

Sleepy Creek was quiet late at night, especially in the suburbs. The wrought-iron lampposts cast vignettes of light on the sidewalk, but I avoided those, sticking on the path, but keeping out of the light for the most part. Just in case someone glanced out of their window and caught sight of me—always a possibility in a town like this.

People didn't pick up on gossip, they went out looking for it. I didn't blame them for the most part. The town didn't even have a cinema, let alone a mall. What else were people supposed to do in their spare time?

Apart from murdering innocent art dealers.

I checked my watched and whistled under my breath. It was already past 11pm, and most of the lights in these houses were off. Here and there, the odd TV flickered between a set of curtains, or I caught a glimpse of someone in the kitchen, having a late night snack.

The air was still, though, and the sky was cloudless overhead, stars sparkling in the inky black, the moon high above and heading toward full.

My mother had always said the full moon made people crazy. After years working homicide, I'd figured out that it wasn't the moon that made them that way.

Then again, I was the one stalking down the town's streets in the dead of the night.

I turned the corner and entered Rich Combes' street.

The husband. The potential murderer. The affair-haver. OK, so maybe the last one wasn't exactly the best label I'd come up with, but it was accurate according to Mona and her gang of gossips.

The house was meant to be at the end of the street, on the right. Number 53 Baker.

I made a beeline for it and approached the front garden. The doctor didn't have a fence, but the grass itself had been well-looked after, and the stepping stone path that led to the front porch was clear by the moonlight.

The lights were on in the living room at the front of the house, and a shadow moved over the curtains.

He was awake.

I'd come to stake the place out, perhaps to spy on his activities, certainly not to intrude or rifle through his trash. Or break-in. *Then why are you even considering it?*

I made my way up the path, keeping to the stones so I wouldn't leave any marks behind— the grass might be wet. People in Sleepy Creek took their horticulture seriously.

My footsteps creaked on the wooden porch steps, and I froze.

But no, the TV flashed and blared on in the living room, and nothing had moved in the house.

I made it to the porch, then headed over to the window and peered into it. It was harmless, of course. *Harmlessly illegal as you're trespassing.* But I had to do whatever it took to get to the bottom of this one.

Twelve years ago, I'd been clueless and I'd let an even more clueless cop take on my mother's case and never solve it. I couldn't rest until Sleepy Creek was safe again.

Since when do you care about this small town?

The crunch of tires sounded from the road, and I crouched down lower, avoiding the beams from a... SUV!

The mistress!

I backed away from the living room window and pressed myself into the darkest corner of the porch, eyes peeled. This might be my moment.

Would the mistress reveal herself? Come right up to the door and knock? And then Rich would open and...

The car door slammed, and a figure emerged from within. They straightened, standing in front of the car for a moment and waved. It was just enough time to give me a glimpse of their face.

My stomach sank.

It wasn't the mistress.

It was the doctor himself. Getting out of the mistress's car? But if that was the case, who was inside Rich's house?

The lights were on inside the car, and the woman driving it turned her head, revealing a face covered in wrinkles, eyes hidden behind her glasses.

Elizabeth? Elizabeth is the mistress?

I kept low and waited, hoping against all hope that he wouldn't spot me crouched next to his porch swing.

He came across the garden, took the stepping stone path up to the porch, humming under his breath. Hardly the behavior of a grieving husband. Rich bounded up the steps and headed for the front door.

A crash rang out inside, and he froze.

I stiffened too.

"What on earth?" Rich murmured, and placed his hand on the doorknob.

My better instincts kicked in.

"Don't," I hissed.

Rich jolted and spun toward me.

I rose from the corner. "I don't know who's in there, Rich, but I wouldn't go in if I were you. Why don't you call the cops?"

The living room lights clicked off, plunging us both into darkness.

"What are you doing here?"

"That's a discussion for later. Clearly, there are more pressing matters at hand. Like the intruder in your house?"

"You mean your friend?" he asked.

"How might they be my friend?"

"Do you think I was born yesterday, Miss Watson? You interrogate me at my office, set your evil little cat on me, and now I find you outside my home while there's a break-in in progress."

"Firstly, Curly Fries is anything but little, and secondly, I swear, I had nothing to do with this. I heard a commotion so I came up here to check everything was all right. I was walking home from a late shift."

Another bang sounded inside, this one closer to the front hall.

"Get back," I whispered. "You don't know who might be in there."

Rich did as he was told, fumbling his cell-phone out of his pocket.

The door slammed open, and a figure darted out and across the porch. They wore a long black cloak and a balaclava.

"Hey!" I yelled. "Stop right there."

But the intruder was already off down the path.

"Hey, get back here." I ran after them, pumping my hands back and forth.

But it was already too late. They had

reached the street and sprinted off down it. In the blink of an eye, the intruder was gone, leaving behind a faint scent I couldn't quite place.

Rich huffed up behind me and stopped on the sidewalk. "Who was it? Did you see?"

"No."

Rich didn't stick around for much longer. He hurried back to his house.

I followed, rapping my knuckles against the door as I entered the short hallway at the front of the house. "Rich? Are you OK?"

"I'm in here," the doctor called.

I walked into the living room and stopped, peering around in the darkness. The room was a mess. Cushions had been ripped from the sofa and torn open. The bookcase had been emptied out, and the pages of its books scattered here and there. The TV had been left untouched, though, still flashing images on mute.

"It's ruined," Rich said, softly. "Everything is ruined."

"I'm so sorry. I wish I could have done something to help."

"You've done enough," he replied, and I wasn't sure if he meant it in a good or bad way. "What do I do now?"

"Listen, Rich, I have to go." I backed up a step. If Balle caught me here, I'd be in a world of trouble. "But my suggestion is that you call the cops and tell them what happened. All right?"

He met my gaze, blankly. "All right."

"Take care." And then I dipped out of the living room and the house itself, and made for the street. I'd gotten what I'd come for—more insight into Rich's relationship with Haley—and a little something I hadn't bargained on.

Whoever had wanted Haley dead, they were still around. That or she'd hidden what the intruder wanted in the house, and they couldn't find it.

But what was it?

And how could it possibly be worth killing someone over?

❦ 16 ❦

The following day at the Burger Bar was mostly a haze. I couldn't get thoughts of what had happened out of my head, and I half-expected Balle to come charging into the restaurant and tell me I was under arrest for interfering in his investigation.

But he didn't materialize, and as the morning wound on, I relaxed into the routine of serving delicious burgers to the many locals of Sleepy Creek. Mona didn't make a reappearance either. And neither did Dr. Rich.

Had he even called the cops?

Something like that would have been news in the restaurant. Another break-in so soon after Haley's murder? People would fit those puzzle pieces together, real quick.

But the talk was about Jerry Lee, as it had been the day before.

After the morning folks were gone, I returned to the front counter with my tray and put it down then scanned the tables I had left.

Only two—and Martin was due to come in and take the next shift. I would have a break, and he would take control of the restaurant and run it like he always did. The man was a machine. I didn't know how he did it.

Then again, everybody had different gifts in life. Mine was sticking my nose where it didn't belong and solving cases for it.

The bell above the door tinkled, and Missi entered the store. She spotted me, pointed to her usual booth then dragged her feet over to it and plopped down.

Missi wasn't particularly chipper on the

best of days, but she seemed positively exhausted now.

I joined her and sat when she gestured. "You all right?" I asked.

"Gee, Watson, I don't know. How do I look to you?" She had dark rings under her eyes, and her silver curls were falling from their usual up do. A smear of grime on her pants suit, too. That wasn't like her. Missi and Vee were both neat.

"Spring cleaning?"

"Try spring stacking," she replied.

"What do you mean?"

"I told you we've been having clients over, yes?"

"Yes."

"Well, we've collected several antiques. Several too many. Virginia is insisting that we keep them upstairs until we can sell them all, but it's driving me crazy."

"What types of things have you collected?"

"Everything from grandfather clocks to jewelry to antique breakfronts to..."

Something twigged in my mind, and I tuned out Missi's litany. "Wait, go back. You mentioned jewelry?"

"Yeah, and so? Are you interested in buying a few pieces? I'll admit you need the gussying up, dear. You're never going to attract that detective Balle looking like that."

I focused on the grains of information in the sentence, rather than the jibe at the end.

Jewelry. I'd heard it several times this week.

Haley's house had been broken into, and her costume jewelry had been stolen.

Haley had been upset because she'd lost her ring.

An image her rose from my memory—before she'd taken a look at the antique box, she'd been fidgeting a lot. Touching her finger again and again. *Because she was missing a ring.*

But what was to say that the jewelry that had gone missing had somehow wound up in Missi and Vee's house? And how would it have gotten there, unless Haley had dropped it on a visit.

"How close were you with Haley?" I asked.

Missi's eyebrows rose. "What's that look on your face, Watson?"

"Tell me, please. How close were you with her? Did she ever come up to your apartment?"

"Maybe, once or twice. The last time was about two weeks before the murder. Why do you ask?"

"What kinds of jewelry have you been keeping up there?"

"We don't keep jewelry." Missi rubbed the wrinkles on her forehead. "We just have a few pieces that were sold to us and one that Virginia found the other day."

"Where?"

"Good heavens, what's gotten into you? You're like a dog with a bone."

"Just answer the question."

"It was a ring," Missi said. "Chunky

looking affair. We're not sure where it came from."

The suspicion that had been wedged in my mind took form. Shadows became clearer. Someone had broken into Haley's house. Her costume jewelry had gone missing, but they clearly hadn't found what they were looking for.

They'd gone back last night and stolen nothing.

Was it possible that Haley's ring hadn't been stolen, but she'd lost it instead? But why did the killer, or the burglar, want it?

Missi cleared her throat. "What's an old woman got to do to get served around here?"

"Where's Virginia?" I asked.

"At home. She's organizing. She loves organizing." Missi rolled her eyes. "And I love burgers, so how about you go get me a—"

I struggled out of my seat. "We have to go."

"What?"

"Right now. You and me, we have to go." I stripped off my apron and charged to the counter at the back of the restaurant.

Grizzy looked up as I approached. "Chris?"

"I'll be back later. I have to go. OK?"

"Where are you—?"

I walked off. I couldn't get the thoughts straight yet, and I needed all my investigative brainpower to focus on this. Missi was out of the booth, now, frowning at me, her back ever so slightly hunched.

"You'd better have a darn good reason for pulling me away from my brunch."

I hurried out into the street then took off toward Terrible Two's Antiques, my stomach burning. Missi matched my stride, huffing out breaths. "What's going on, Watson?"

"It's the ring. There's something about it. Something ... I just know it's connected. Haley was at your place, she lost her ring. That's what he wants. He. She said it was a man who did this."

Could it have been Jerry Lee?

"You're not making much sense."

It was a miracle I was making any. My mind whirred too fast for my mouth to keep up. My pace quickened, and Missi lagged behind. The closer we got to the antique store, the faster my heart beat.

What if I was right? What if the twins were in danger because of Haley's ring?

But then, what if I was wrong? I was out on a limb here. There were plenty of other suspects, and why had the murderer chosen to attack Haley in broad daylight?

How could he possibly have predicted that she would have been in the antique store?

I turned the corner, Missi hot on my heels, and pulled up short.

The road in front of the store bustled with activity. Two police cruisers were parked on the verge, and an ambulance had pulled up between them. A woman on a stretcher, oxygen mask over her face, was rolled toward the waiting open doors of the van.

I lifted my hand to shield my eyes from the sun.

"No!" Missi cried. "It's Virginia!"

And she was right. Vee was on the stretcher, her arms crossed over her chest.

"Vee!" I took off running toward the cluster of people. "Let me through. Let me through, I'm a police officer." I squeezed through the crowd of people, pressing bodies to the side.

Finally, I burst through.

The doors of the ambulance closed. I ran forward and grabbed for one of the handles, but a hand tugged on my arm. It was tan and strong.

"Let go of me. That's Virginia in there," I said, and turned an angry gaze toward the person who'd restrained me.

"I know, Christie." Balle's brown eyes greeted me. "She's OK. She's going to the hospital. You can follow behind, if you want."

"What's going on?" Missi squeezed

through as the ambulance drove off, its lights flashing but the siren silent. "Where are you taking my sister?"

"Ride with me," Balle said. "I'll explain on the way."

❦ 17 ❧

Missi had already gone into the hospital room in Logan's Rest and seated herself at Virginia's side. The plum-haired twin was out cold.

Balle had broken it down for us in the car, briefly. She'd been attacked in the living room upstairs. Struck from behind with a heavy object. Witnesses had spotted a man in black wearing a balaclava fleeing the scene. The antiques had been tipped over, torn apart, and smashed in places, some of the jewelry had been taken.

The attacker had been looking for something.

"Are you OK?" The detective walked down the hall toward me, his polished shoes clicking on the linoleum. He held out a steaming Styrofoam cup. "Best I can do, right now. Hospital coffee is always a winner."

I took a sip and grimaced. "Funny, I've never tasted sarcasm before, but I think this is it."

He nodded toward the doors. "What did the doctors say?"

"That she should be fine. That she should wake up soon. That it's probably just a concussion, and that she's very lucky to be all right." I turned on Balle. "What were you thinking making an arrest so soon?"

"Pardon me?" His gruff tone reemerged.

"You had to have some kind of evidence to arrest Jerry Lee, but it's clear you jumped the gun."

"How so?"

"Look at her in there." I motioned with

my cup. "Do you think this was a random attack? Or just a burglary? Come on, put two and two together, detective." Unless Jerry Lee had been working with someone on the outside. Or Rich had faked the break-in at his house? It would explain why he hadn't reported it.

"Watson, you're about as clear as a slice of chocolate pie most of the time, but you're outdoing yourself right now."

"Don't tell me you don't know about the break-in at Haley's house. The missing costume jewelry? And the thief strikes a second time at Missi and Vee's place and just so happens to take the same thing?"

"I know about those events, yes, but how do you know about them?" His dark eyebrows drew inward.

I was too invested in the outcome of the case to care about getting in trouble now. "How do you think I know? Because I've been checking it out. I had my suspicions the minute you arrested Jerry Lee, and they're confirmed, now. All I don't know is what evidence you have to hold him in jail when he's so clearly not the culprit. Or not the only culprit."

"This is an ongoing investigation, Christie. I'm going to have to report your involvement to your superior if you continue in this—"

"Then report me," I said. "Go ahead. I'm not going to sit by and watch while the people I care about are hurt." Goodness, I cared about them? Of course I did. The twins had become a fixture in the Burger Bar, and they'd come to help Grizzy and I the last time we'd been in trouble.

"Watson, don't do this. You're going to regret it."

I raised a finger and poked him in his muscly chest. "The only thing I regret is not involving myself sooner. You owe me an explanation."

"I don't owe you anything."

"Then don't pretend that you care about Missi and Vee. You're the one who put Jerry in jail while some masked attacker is still on the loose."

"Christie, relax." Balle took hold of my arms. I let him. "You're assuming that the attacker is the murderer, and we don't know that for sure. Jerry's been arraigned for a good reason."

Poor Grizzy had gone to visit him. The judge had denied bail as he was a 'flight risk.' Ridiculous.

"What reason?" I asked. "What evidence do you have?"

His hands were tucked under my elbows now, and his eyes flicked back and forth. "You know I can't reveal that and jeopardize my case. And getting you involved jeopardizes your future in Boston."

"Liam."

He was quiet for a moment. "Fingerprints on the box and inside it. And a note, also with his fingerprints on it. That's all I can say."

"What did the note say? Please, tell me."

A muscle worked in his jaw. "I've got what

you lost. Meet me at Terrible Two's at 9am. It's inside the box."

I inhaled sharply.

"What?"

"The ring."

"What are you talking about?" Balle asked.

I broke it down for him, quickly. The fact that Haley's ring had gone missing, the break-ins I'd witnessed, and my suspicion that Haley had wanted that ring back, that it was important somehow, and that the killer had used that against her. He'd wanted her to open the box.

But if that was the case, how had Jerry Lee been involved? He hadn't even known Haley.

So he said.

Liam listened calmly to everything then finally released my arms.

I touched the spots where his hands had been, absently. "Don't you see? It's not over yet. The killer has to be out there somewhere, and they want that ring too."

"Christie, I respect that you were a detective."

"I *am* one. I wasn't fired."

"Sure. I respect that, but you can't get involved like this, and you certainly can't jump to conclusions based on a few strands of information. If there's some connection here, you have to trust that Arthur and I will find it."

"I didn't say I don't trust you." I glanced into the room. Virginia's eyes had finally opened, and she gave Missi a weak smile. The sisters held hands.

"Then let me do my job. Let me check out the leads."

But how was I supposed to do that when the officers moved at a glacial pace? They had red tape to contend with that I didn't.

"Christie," Liam said. "I need you to stay out of this. I need to make sure that you don't—"

"I heard you the first time." But I couldn't make any promises. I had to get this sorted out before it was too late.

Who knew who might be next in Sleepy Creek?

No one. Because I'm going to find the killer and stop them.

And I knew exactly where to start looking.

❧ 18 ❧

Balle had given me a ride back to Sleepy Creek and dropped me off in front of the Burger Bar with the warning to stay out of trouble. The sun was low on the horizon, and Grizzy, bless her soul, was inside toiling away.

Likely, she'd heard about the news through the gossip vine, but she hadn't managed to get free to go visit Vee.

I didn't have time to stop by and placate her.

I waited until Balle's cruiser had disappeared around the corner then took off running down the street.

A few of the locals jumped out of my path as I blew by.

"Hey, slow down before you hurt somebody!" a woman yelled.

I kept going, pushing myself to go faster and faster, my lungs burning from the effort. At last, I thundered around the corner and came upon Terrible Two's Antiques. I headed into the alley and took the rickety metal fire escape two stairs at a time.

The door to their upstairs apartment was locked, but the window had been broken. I reached in and unlatched the door then let myself into the kitchen. I hit the switch on the wall, and light filled the kitchen.

Everything in here was in order. But what about in the next room? I didn't have time to worry about police procedures now. If there was the off chance that I might find a clue here, or even the ring that Haley had lost, I had to take it.

I walked through the kitchen, checked the corners just in case and shook my head at myself. It would be idiotic of the attacker to come back here now, assuming he hadn't gotten what he was looking for in the first place.

The lights were off in the house, and I clicked them on one room at a time then started my search. I began in the bedrooms—two of them, each with a single bed. One was definitely Missi's style, with a poster of Idris Elba on the wall, a Bible on the desk and the walls a deep navy blue.

The other, Vee's, bore floral wall paper, a dresser with a mirror that was big enough to reflect the other half of the room and a bed neatly made, a lone brown teddy bear resting on the pillows.

I chewed the inside of my cheek. Poor Vee.

This time it wasn't my fault. If Balle had followed the more obvious leads, this would never have happened.

I had to keep telling myself that. And that I would get to the bottom of this before the killer struck again.

The killer.

Could it be Rich working with someone else?

Or Elizabeth doing the same? Even Jerry Lee? And what about the old antique dealer who had threatened him, William the Third?

What if it was someone else entirely? Someone who had slipped beneath the radar?

I headed into the living room and found the mess I'd expected.

The grandfather clock was on its side, the polished wood cracked. Books had been strewn across the room, the cushion cases emptied, and an antique statute broken open. It was the same picture of chaos I'd seen over at Rich's place.

I started on the left side of the room and worked my way over to the right. I had to try, at least. I got on all fours and scoured the living room, searched beneath the sofa and be-

tween the antiques, those that had been ruined and those that hadn't.

After fifteen minutes of searching, I
straightened and brushed off my hands.

The ring wasn't here.

Not in this room.

But that didn't mean it wasn't in the
apartment.

"If I was Virginia, where would I put a
mystery ring?" I chewed on my bottom lip.
"Think, Christie, think." I clicked my fingers.
"The bedrooms."

The twins would have to forgive me for
rifling through their things later on. This was
for a good cause—making sure that neither of
them were attacked, ever again.

I scuttled through to the hall and entered
the first bedroom. It was Missi's. I opened the
Bible, checked the pages then went through
her desk drawers. Nothing. I was hesitant to
check her dresser, just in case I ran into deli-
cates that weren't too... well, delicate.

I entered Virginia's room instead and

headed for her dressing table. I sat down at it, frowning at myself in the mirror. Dark semi-circles beneath the eyes, messy hair, definitely don't care, and not a hint of a mascara.

What would mom say?

I scanned the table.

A pink, heart-shaped box rested on the varnished surface. "What's this?" I muttered.

I lifted the box and clicked it open. And there, within it, sat the ring. It had to be the ring. It was gaudy and ugly—a massive yellow gemstone sparkling in a bronze setting, with two smaller purple gems along the band.

What was so special about this ring?

I lifted it out of the jewelry box and placed it in the center of my palm, tilting it this way and that. The dark etchings on the underside of the ring caught my gaze.

Press me.

The words sat against the circle of brass behind the gemstone. I extended my finger.

"Don't do it, Miss Watson," a woman spoke behind me. "If you want to live."

❧ 19 ❧

I met her gaze in the mirror.

She wore her hair dark, had her uniform on, perfectly pressed. She held a gun and aimed it at my back. Arm was steady. She'd done that before. Perhaps, even shot someone before.

But that wasn't the worst of it, not by far.

She was the last person I'd expected to see here.

"You," I said, wracking my brain for the name that was on the tip of my tongue. "You're Elizabeth's servant."

"Assistant," the young woman snapped. "And the name is Isabella."

I stared at her, dumbfounded. I had expected William to be the killer, not her. This didn't add up. She wasn't involved with antiques, she certainly wasn't having an affair with Richard, unless ... had Elizabeth been helping her assistant have an affair with Dr. Rich?

"Dad," Isabella called, over her shoulder. "She's in here."

Footsteps shuffled through the house, and William Radisson the Third entered the bedroom. He was taller than his daughter, but their noses were exactly the same, as were their bushy eyebrows, drawn inward as they studied me.

"She's got the ring," Isabella said.

"Ah, very good. Then she'll have to give it to me, won't she? Yes, dear, you will."

I watched them in the mirror, hesitant to make any sudden movements in case Isabella decided to fire off a shot.

Think, Christie, think. What is this about?

"Why do you want the ring?" I asked. "Why did you kill Haley for it?"

"Haley was a smart girl. Far too smart for her own good. If she'd kept her nose out of our business, everything would have been fine. Hand it over." Isabella put out her hand. "Now."

"Now, now, Izzy darling, there's no need to be tetchy."

Who even says tetchy?

"Dad, she's got to give it up. I'll kill you if you don't," Isabella said, directing the last sentence at me.

"Put the gun down, Izzy. She's no danger to us, and if she gives us any trouble, I've got a solution to that." William lifted a syringe from his pocket and took a piece of cork off the sharp end. "See this? Cyanide. One little squirt and you're done. Silent, deadly, and impressive. Easily accessible too. If you have friends in the right places." He laughed. "Now, how about you turn around and give us that ring."

"What's inside it?" I asked, turning slowly on the chair. I rose, but kept the ring in my palm. "What are you hiding?"

"I don't suppose there's any harm in you knowing." William held the syringe upright and tapped its side.

"Dad, there's no time for this. They might have followed her here."

"Don't be ridiculous, Izzy. The police in this town are entirely blind. They wouldn't know a murderer if I walked up and injected them with poison."

The temptation to press the button on the inside of the ring was almost overwhelming. There had to be a way out.

I scanned the room while William and Izzy argued.

A dull thump sounded in the house, but neither of the murderers seemed to notice.

I held my breath and pressed my finger to

the inside of the ring. It clicked against my thumb, and the gem on the front popped free on a tiny hinge. I lifted it and slipped out a tiny SD card from within, then closed the ring silently.

"—tell her our motivation for doing anything. She doesn't need to know. She's a nobody."

"I'm a police officer," I said, as I slipped the SD card into my back pocket, still holding the now empty ring in my hand for them to see. "From Boston. Not a nobody. If you kill me, a lot of people are going to start asking questions."

They exchanged a glance.

"Just give us the ring and nobody has to get hurt," William said.

"You can have it." I cocked my hand back and threw it directly at Isabella. The ring struck her on the forehead and *plinked* to the carpeted floor. It rolled underneath the bed.

"You horrible witch," Izzy said. "That hurt."

"Never mind that, darling, get down there and get that ring."

Isabella dove down onto the floor while William advanced, aiming the syringe at me, his eyes narrowing.

"Now, now, dear, hold still. This won't hurt a bit. Actually, that's a lie. It will hurt a lot."

I backed up and hit the dresser.

"I've got it!" Izzy cried from underneath the bed. "I've got the ring. You can kill her, dad."

William lifted the syringe.

I sucked in a breath and braced myself.

Detective Balle stepped through the bedroom door, his gun up. "Freeze, Sleepy Creek police. Drop the weapon, right now! Drop it or I'll shoot."

William gasped and let the syringe fall to the carpet.

"Watch out," I said. "The one on the floor has a gun."

And that was it.

Detective Cotton charged into the room

and took William into custody. Balle disarmed Isabella and escorted her out. And me? I was alive with a back pocket full of evidence, and a hankering to see the murderers put away for a long, long time.

❧ 20 ☙

"I can't believe it's true," Grizzy said, as she tugged off one of her soil-streaked gloves. She wiped her forehead with the back of her hand.

We were crouched in the front yard, beneath the windows, planting poppies as I'd promised at the beginning of the week. It was a mundane task after so much action the night before, but it helped settle my nerves.

"They were con-artists. Apparently, this Isabella traveled from town to town seeking out rich old ladies or gentlemen and would then start working for them."

"And then what?" Grizzy asked.

"She would ingratiate herself with the rich woman and then introduce them to William in some manner or the other." I fumbled in the soil.

Grizzy shook her head. "No, no, not like that. Oh for heaven's sake, Chris, just let me do it." She swept the trowel out of my hand and set to work.

The sun baked the backs of our necks, but shoot, I was happy for it. At least, I had a neck to bake. It had come close to being the real end for me last night. I was lucky that Balle hadn't trusted me not to get involved and had followed me back to Missi and Vee's apartment.

"But I don't understand how Haley is involved in all of this? Or what this had to do with antiques or Jerry Lee?"

"In truth, it had nothing to do with antiques. Haley just happened to be there when

Isabella was and realized that something was up. Apparently, she started keeping track of the finances and the strange things that both William and Isabella were doing. She stored all the information on an SD card and hid that in the ring. The same ring that she accidentally lost at Missi and Vee's place the last time she visited."

"Good heavens. So that's why they killed her."

"Yeah. They realized she could uncover the trail of thievery and destruction they'd left across the State. William wasn't even an antique collector. He just played the part so he could get closer to Elizabeth."

"That's sad."

"Very. Poor Elizabeth. She's the real sufferer in all of this. And Haley too."

"But what about the affair with Rich?"

"There was no affair," I said, and rolled my eyes. "That was just hearsay from Mona Jonah. Rich was just trying to be supportive of the old woman, who's pretty ill. He's a doctor.

And Jerry Lee? He was a convenient scapegoat for the murder, since he traveled in the same circles. My theory is William wanted to pin it on him."

"Of course." Grizzy finished planting another poppy plant and sat back on her haunches, peering at me, her golden hair glistening in the sun. "I can't believe all the drama. Who would have thought it would all come down to this? Two con-artists, a rich woman, and Haley caught in the middle because she was trying to be a Good Samaritan."

What she'd been trying to do was investigations of her own when she should have gone to the police from the start.

Ring a bell, Watson?

The front door opened, and we both turned toward it. Jerry Lee came down the steps, carrying his leather suitcase and bearing a smile. "Hello," he said.

"Morning, Jerry Lee. Sleep all right?" I asked.

"The best night's sleep I've had in a week.

I'm a free man. And I'll tell you, as much as I love this little town, I can't wait to get out of it." Jerry came over, bobbing up and down as he walked. He stopped and offered me a hand.

I got up, pulled my gardening glove off, and shook it. "Sorry, I'm clammy from all the menial labor."

"Menial labor." Grizzy snorted. "It's planting flowers, not laying a railroad."

"Leaving already?" I asked.

"You bet I am. Gosh, I don't think I'll be back for a few years, now. Sleepy Creek and Jerry Lee Lewis don't mix."

"Great balls of fire?" Griselda grinned, rising too.

"I can't thank you enough, Christie." Jerry pumped my arm up and down. "If you hadn't solved this case, I would still be in jail. I just … thank you."

"It wasn't all me," I said. "Grizzy helped. And Detective Balle was there too."

"Somebody call my name?" Liam stood near the front gate, dapper in his uniform.

The police cruiser was parked in the street. "Can you spare a moment, Christie? We need to talk."

"Oh boy," I muttered. "Wish me luck."

"Good luck!" Grizzy called, a little too loudly, and my cheeks grew red as the tomato slices Jarvis had put on the burgers this week.

"And that's my cue to leave. Bye, Griz. I'll see you at the next family reunion. Bye!" Jerry Lee rushed off, opened the gate and slipped out of it, giving the detective a wide berth. He was off up the street and heading for the bus stop at a blistering pace.

Who could blame the guy? He'd had one heck of a week.

"Christie?" Liam prompted.

"Right. Yeah. Coming." I stepped out of the garden and walked to his cruiser with him.

He leaned against it, his tan forearms folded and tilted his head to one side. "Know why I'm here?"

"I'm guessing it's not to thank me for

finding the evidence you needed to lock two megalomaniacs behind bars."

"You've got spunk, Watson, I'll give you that."

"As long as you don't give me a prison sentence along with it," I replied.

"You think I'm here to arrest you?" A smile cracked his lips.

"I did interfere in an ongoing investigation."

"Hmm. You helped set it right, actually." He shook his head. "I shouldn't even be saying that, but it is what it is. That note I told you about? It was a very good forgery of Jerry Lee's handwriting. How they managed to get his fingerprint on it, I'll never know, but my best guess is they stole a piece of paper he'd already touched. All of that, and I would have been nowhere near solving the case if it wasn't for you."

My stomach started its gymnastics again. "Oh."

"So thank you for that. I appreciate it. If

you weren't on sabbatical, I'd ask you to con-
sult for us when stuff like this happened."

"It was nothing. I mean... Yeah. I know I
shouldn't get involved, I just—Griselda was
upset, and it's like a compulsion for me. I need
the truth."

"You miss it, don't you? Being back
home?"

"Not so much the city. I kind of like it
here," I said, "but the investigations? Yeah,
I do."

Liam's expression darkened. "I had to
write you into my report, Christie. And if
need be, they might call you as a witness. We
want to put those two away for a long time.
You know what this means, don't you?"

"The Chief will find out," I said.

"Yes. I'm sorry."

"I made this choice. If I get punished for
it, then I'll accept those consequences." But
my stomach sank. If I got fired for this, my
badge taken away, it would eat at me for the
rest of my life.

I hadn't even touched my mother's case yet.

Liam exhaled. "I can't lie in my report," he said. "If I could..."

"No, don't say that. Look, I'll deal with what comes next. I understand."

The detective lingered. He opened his mouth then shut it again. Finally, he pushed off from the car. "All right, Watson," he said, at last. "I'll see you around."

"See you."

He got into his cruiser, and I backed up toward the fence, watching as the car drove off down the road, his silhouette stiff inside it.

"What was that about?" Grizzy popped up behind me. "Are you in trouble?"

"When am I not in trouble?"

"True." She chuckled. "Chris, are you OK?"

"Yoo-hoo!" The shout came from down the street, and a grin started up on my lips.

Missi and Virginia came toward us, arm-in-arm, a spring in their steps. Vee had been released yesterday with pills for her head and instructions to take it easy. They were both healthy and alive.

The sun shone overhead. Curly Fries wound through the garden and chased butterflies. Ray shouted at his TV next door, and Grizzy had managed to smear soil across her forehead in a big brown streak.

"Am I OK?" I asked, under my breath. "I've never been better."

Whatever came next, I had these people to lean on.

For the first time since I'd come back to Sleepy Creek, I was at home.

Catch up with more of Christie's adventures in the next book in the series. The Chicken Burger Murder is available at all major retailers.

THANK YOU, READER!

Thank you so much for reading Christie's story. If you enjoyed the book, I would be honored if you left a review. They're basically the crispy fries of an author's career. (I know, I should probably stop with the puns—ha!)

MORE FOR YOU...

Sign up to my mailing list and receive updates on future releases, as well as a **FREE** copy of *The Hawaiian Burger Murder* and *The Fully Loaded Burger Murder.*

They are two short cozy mysteries featuring characters from the Burger Bar Mystery series.

Click here to join the mailing list.

Made in the USA
Middletown, DE
30 July 2023

35943846R00135